RK - ret

Pat
No

1

Kathy!
Thank you for all of
your support. All the best
wishes,
Victoria
Parker

Special thanks to those who backed this project:

Marci E.

Cindy E.

Mark K.

Christin P.

Roberta B.

Jade F.

Krystal K.

&

Tim & Pam P.

This book is for you.

I couldn't have done it without you!!

Thank you so much for your support!

Forward:

Some of these stories have been published elsewhere while others haven't been seen outside of my classroom or even by anyone but myself. Some have led to longer stories while others were told just for the fun of it. Some are humorous while others are dark. Before each story, I've written a small preface to tell you a bit of the story's background. I hope you enjoy reading them as much as I've enjoyed writing them.

6

TABLE OF CONTENTS

8

THE SPACES BETWEEN

Originally written for a sci-fi anthology that never came to fruition, I have since released this short story in e-book form through Amazon. My favorite part of the story is that I got to make a world where trees were blue. So, to my kindergarten teacher who once wrote on one of my art projects that there was no such thing as blue trees, I say, they do exist in worlds that you just couldn't imagine.

Mankind has been theorizing for centuries about life on other planets and how first contact will be made. Vast spaceships appearing from the sky with creatures either far superior or far more aggressive than our own species. Most bent on destruction or enslavement. Some coming in peace only to face prejudice among the humans.

They were all wrong.

***

Cali Marks brought down the axe with all the force a five foot, one inch linguist could muster. Surprisingly, it was enough to split the stubborn log in two. Cali laid the axe aside and stooped to retrieve the pieces. She pushed absently at a strand of dark brown hair that had managed to escape from her waist-length braid, leaving a smudge of dirt across her cheek. She didn't mind. The physical work was exactly what she needed to get her mind off of the mess she called her life. Her green eyes clouded over momentarily before she shoved her thoughts aside and focused on the task at hand.

By the time she was twenty-four, Cali had earned a double doctorate in Greek and Italian, was fluent in twelve other languages and able to hold basic conversations in almost twenty more. It was this skill that had allowed Cali to travel all over the world and had, just three days shy of her twenty-fifth birthday, led her into the arms of Jabir Nekkar, a Middle Eastern prince and heir to one of the world's largest fortunes. They'd had a whirlwind romance, covered by every media outlet from Europe to Asia to the US. When Jabir had proposed only six months into their relationship, the nations swooned. Then, four days after Cali's twenty-sixth birthday, with half the world watching, Jabir left Cali at the altar. Cali's best friend, Jaycee, had offered the Colorado cabin as a means of escape from the hounding press and Cali immediately took it. That had been two weeks ago.

Cali dumped her armload of wood into the rack next to the fireplace and headed back outside for more. The sun was already setting and she still had a few more loads before she'd have enough firewood to last her through the night. Autumn nights in the Rockies could be cold.

She was only a few feet from the cabin's door when the orange-red sky ripped in two with a sound like thunder. Something tumbled through the dark expanse, hurtling towards the ground even as the torn edges of the heavens slammed back together. Cali stared at the place where the strange object had disappeared into the trees, internally debating the wisdom of investigating while another part of her mind tried to rationalize what she'd just witnessed. The innate curiosity that had driven her to study exotic and dying languages won out and she hesitated only long enough to grab a flashlight before heading into the forest.

Cali'd always had a good sense of direction and it served her well as she wove her way through the woods without any clear path or guidance. It was darker under the cover of the trees but, without really understanding why she was doing it, Cali kept the flashlight off. The acrid tang of ozone was her first indication that she was close; the second was the sound of someone or something in pain. Cali moved faster, ignoring the small portion of her brain that cautioned against getting nearer to whatever was making that pitiful noise. She took a few more steps and found herself in a clearing, though not a natural one. The tops of several trees at the perimeter had been sheared off and whatever had been at ground level was lost in a blackened indentation. At the center of the circle was a figure.

As she drew closer, Cali heard a gasp escape her lips. Her mind immediately returned to a childhood of Sunday mornings in church, unable to process what she was seeing in any other way. Waves of silver-blond hair around a face that was both pretty and masculine at the same time. Golden skin gleaming from beneath tattered black cloth. And, stretched out underneath a lean, muscled frame, wings. A second look revealed that the wings were not the pure white depicted on angelic beings, but a combination silver and gold that matched hair and skin, tipped with a dark color indistinguishable in the darkness.

"*Khnraigh cabhdrum m.*"

Cali instinctively knew that they were words, but they were a language she'd never encountered. It didn't matter, though, the message was clear enough. Whoever, or whatever, was lying there was in pain and needed help. She took a few more steps forward, venturing onto the charred ground. Now she could see that one of the wings was bent at a strange angle and patches of skin were covered in a dark liquid.

In the same soothing voice one would use for a wounded animal, Cali spoke. "It's okay. I'm here to help you. It'll all be okay."

Cali wasn't sure how she managed to get the stranger back to the cabin on her own. He was at least a foot and a half taller than she and barely conscious, but she somehow found herself lowering the man onto the couch as gently as possible. As she straightened, she could feel his blood against her skin, slippery and warm, soaking into her clothes. She looked down and caught her breath. What she hadn't been able to seen in the darkening night was clearly visible under the soft lamplight of the living room. The blood staining her hands and shirt was a deep, rich blue.

"This is bad." Cali whispered, eyes wide as she stared at her hands. "This is really bad."

"*Khnraigh cabhdrum m.*" The stranger on the couch opened his eyes and looked up at Cali. She swallowed hard, unsure which was effecting her more: the fact that his eyes had a ring of dark chocolate brown surrounding a ring of bright sapphire blue, or the pain and fear in those eyes. No matter what he was, she knew she had to help him.

Cali knelt next to the couch, taking the stranger's hand in her own. "You're safe, and I'm going help you." Whether in response to her tone or as a result of his injuries, the stranger's eyelids closed and his body relaxed. Cali's next words were to herself. "All right, basic first aid. Assess the wounds. Determine which are the most serious. Stop any bleeding."

Cali pushed hair back from the stranger's face. It was unmarked and youthful. She forced herself to continue her examination. She could see now that his shirt was shredded, the shiny black cloth made of material she'd never seen. She retrieved a pair of scissors from the kitchen and carefully cut away the shirt. As the last of the scraps fell away, she clasped her hand to her mouth in horror. Deep lashes, ones that Cali unconsciously associated with a whip, crossed the stranger's chest from right shoulder to left hip and left shoulder to right hip, leaving the center of his torso a ragged, bloody mess. The sight of ruined flesh was enough to break Cali of her shock over the dark blue color of the blood and she immediately hurried to the bathroom for supplies.

Cali worked with careful precision, cleaning and disinfecting each lash, all the while watching her patient for signs of discomfort. He didn't stir as Cali dressed the wounds on his chest before turning her attention to the obviously broken wing. As a child, Cali had once found a chickadee with a broken wing. Her older brother, Ian, had shown her how to immobilize the injury and bind it to allow the bird time to heal. A few weeks later, they'd released the bird back into the sky and watched as it'd flown away. Cali picked up the sheet she'd cut into strips, took a deep breath, and tried to remember everything that her brother had taught her.

***

The hot water washed away the blood, but couldn't scrub clean the images in Cali's head. The wounds had been vicious, intentionally inflicted. And, judging by the fresh scars she'd found on the rest of the stranger's body, not the first he'd endured. Then there was the matter of the wings. Closer examination revealed that they weren't exactly like bird wings, having extra joints that allowed them to fold up in a different manner than Cali had originally thought. The reason for this was soon obvious as Cali stretched out one of the wings to a width of sixteen feet. The length was another issue. Had the stranger been standing, the tips of the lowest feathers would have brushed his calves, making the wings at least as long as Cali was tall. Based on the wing structure, the unknown language and the strange blood, Cali knew that even the seemingly far-fetched idea of human experimentation wouldn't explain her visitor.

"He's an alien." She forced herself to whisper the words and shivered despite the steam rolling off her skin. She toweled off and pulled on the first clothes she laid her hands on, suddenly frantic to reassure herself that she wasn't losing her mind. She breathed a sigh of relief as she entered the living room and saw the figure still lying on the couch.

Cali moved a few steps closer and the stranger stirred. The sharp intake of breath was enough to let Cali know that her patient had regained consciousness. After a moment's hesitation, Cali crossed the room.

"*Shnorolch ognaibh fy haliom m. Aimn enanunn ywe Bren Yev Tuar.*" His voice was weak, but stronger than it had been just hours before.

Cali smiled and shook her head. "I don't know what you're saying."

"*Vorble bhfuydw iye?*" He struggled to sit up, noticing his injuries for the first time. "*Ograibh?*" He pointed at Cali and then at his bandages.

Cali nodded. "Yes, I put those on." She pointed at herself. "Cali Marks."

"Cali Marks." Her name sounded odd on his tongue. He mimicked her movement. "Bren Yev Tuar."

"Bren?" Cali pointed at him again, feeling the familiar excitement at learning a new language. She turned to pull one of the chairs closer to the couch and heard Bren gasp. She spun around, afraid that something had happened.

Bren was staring at her, strange eyes wide, skin paler than it had been moments ago. "*Vorble ywen vochuid verinydd? Vorble bhfuydw iye?*" He gestured as he spoke and Cali suddenly understood what he was asking.

"I don't have wings. I'm not like you." Cali sat down on the chair and leaned forward. "You are on Earth." As she'd done many times before, she linked the question and the answer to bridge the language barrier. "*Vorble bhfuydw iye?* Earth." She repeated the pairing again and saw the realization dawn in his eyes.

"Earth."

Cali nodded, her smile widening. The first breakthrough was always like this, exciting, and leaving her wanting more. Fortunately, her pupil was intelligent and just as eager to learn. For hours, they exchanged words and phrases, until, finally, Bren eyes slipped shut mid-sentence and Cali knew that they'd done enough. She gently tucked a blanket around him and retired to her room. Sleep evaded her as the day's events replayed themselves in her head until, she too, fell asleep.

The sound of the cabin door opening woke Cali. For a moment, she panicked. Then, the events of the previous night came flooding back to her and her panic shifted from concern for her own safety to the well-being of her strange visitor. She rushed out of her room and into the living room.

Bren stood just a few feet away, bare feet just inside the doorframe as he peered up at the rising sun. His right wing was partially extended, the edge pressed against the door. A gentle breeze ruffled Bren's feathers, making the colors dance in the light. He seemed intrigued by the sunlight, but made no move to venture outside.

"Bren?" Cali kept her voice soft so as not to frighten him.

"Cali," Bren smiled as he turned.

"Would you like something to eat?" Cali motioned as she spoke. "Food?"

Bren's smile widened as he replied in careful, accented English, "yes."

As they ate, Cali and Bren continued learning each other's words, both quick enough studies that a story began to unfold.

Bren was, as Cali had suspected, not exactly local. He wasn't quite sure where his home was located in relation to Earth, but it was far enough away that the star charts Cali managed to find online were of no use. *Hailneri*, he explained, had towering tree-like plants that grew hundreds of feet into the air. The soil was poisonous to the touch for the *Hailneri* people and they made their home in the wide expanse of forest and air, which, he explained, was why he hadn't cross the threshold. Travel outside of their world was not common, but not unheard of, though no one, as far as Bren knew, had ever managed to travel outside the solar system. All of the other planets had people like the *Hailneri*, people with wings who lived in the trees. Though different types of wings were not uncommon, Cali was the first that Bren had seen without them. When Cali had inquired about space ships, Bren had no idea of what she meant. The *Hailneri* moved in *ayn tarasanby idwngev* – the spaces between. Cali thought back to what she'd witnessed the day before and nodded her head. She may not have had a grasp of the full science behind it, but she understood the theory well enough.

"Did the," she attempted the words, "*ayn tarasanby idwngey* do that?" She pointed at his chest, his wing.

Bren's face darkened and he shook his head. His unbound wing twitched as if he were nervous. A faint flush crept up his neck, blue rather than red. The spreading color brought heat to Cali's cheeks as she realized that her guest was shirtless. She'd been so fascinated by his words and wings that'd she'd forgotten that only the bandages covered his torso. A second thought occurred on the heels of the first. Nothing she owned would fit him, even without the massive wings attached to his back. She made a mental note to search the cabin for something one of Jaycee's brothers might have left behind.

Cali's chirping ring tone startled them both and she grabbed for her phone, surprised that she had a signal. She didn't recognize the number and was tempted to let the call go to voicemail. She sighed. Only a few people had her new number and she knew that for them to contact her meant that it was something important.

"Hello?"

"Cali Marks?" The voice was unfamiliar and professional.

"Yes?" Cali resisted the urge to be rude.

"My name is Jonathan Brandon. I am President Morgan's Chief of Staff." The seriousness of the man's tone immediately dispelled any doubt Cali might have had to the call's authenticity. "We have a situation, Miss Marks, and it has come to my attention that you are the most qualified in your field."

"I don't understand." Cali could fee the weight of Bren's unusual eyes as he watched her.

"Have you not seen the news today, Miss Marks?" Brandon's voice had gone strangely quiet.

"No, I haven't." Cali glanced at Bren, a sinking feeling in the pit of her stomach as her gaze fell on the bandages.

The words reverberated in Cali's ears as if from far away. Only pieces seeped through as flashes from the previous night replayed in her mind. A strange tear in the sky. Four winged beings appearing, speaking an unknown language. Cali now knew where this conversation was heading, so the invitation wasn't a surprise. Though she wasn't entirely sure 'invitation' was the right word. Brandon's phrasing was a bit stronger. In fact, he didn't so much ask Cali as inform her when the plane would arrive to pick her up from the Denver airport. By the time Cali hung up the phone and turned towards Bren, the visitor was already on his feet.

"Four more *Hailneri* have come." Cali spoke slowly, choosing each word carefully. "I am ordered to go meet with them."

Bren's eyes widened, the alarm in them clear. He began to speak, his words tumbling out faster than Cali could follow. But she didn't need to understand the specifics to know that these other visitors were not friends. She pointed at his chest and wing. After a brief hesitation, Bren nodded, some of the urgency leaving him.

"Bren," Cali took a tentative step forward. "I need you to tell me what happened."

Bren opened his mouth, shook his head and then tried again. Cali could see his struggle to express himself and took a step towards him. "I do not have the words." Bren stood, frustration betrayed by every tense muscle, by his clenched hands.

Then, in a movement so swift that Cali almost didn't see

it, he'd crossed the space between them. He looked down at Cali, his strange eyes darkening. His voice was low. "I can show you." With no regard for his injuries, Bren lifted Cali from her feet and bent his head until his mouth captured hers.

***

The night sky was a rich, emerald green beneath the golden moon. A beautiful night to soar above the pale blue blesindz trees that surrounded the castle. But Bren could not enjoy the night as he fought the urge to beat his wings against the air. Stealth was more important than speed at the moment as he slid from shadow to shadow. He focused on each individual movement, hoping that the intense concentration would drown out the screams that echoed in his ears. Hailneri's king and queen, Ardrom and Kajfryd, strong and true, never faltering even as the captain of the guard did her worst. The brave and lovely Princess Sirtais protecting her sisters to the last. And the twins… Bren's flight faltered as he thought of his youngest sisters, mischievous Maclan and gentle Aladar. Vnaspet had known that the destruction of his family would cause Bren far more pain than any torture even the talented Dazead could imagine. But, as always, Vnaspet had underestimated his cousin. Bren had let his anger fuel him, give him the strength to overpower the newest of the guards, Dazead's little brother, Davannid, and the captain's only weakness. Davannid had been the hostage that had allowed Bren past the outer wall.

Bren winced as a blesindz leaf brushed against the wounds on his chest, the pain pulling his thoughts back to the present. He had no plan, no idea of where to go to hide from his cousin. He could hear the guards behind him, could feel the strain of the past three cycles of abuse and malnourishment wearing on his body. A sudden updraft caught him off guard and he struggled to right himself.

He heard the bone snap moments before he felt the impact of the blesindz tree, the white-hot fire in his wing. He tumbled towards the ground, uninjured wing flailing in vain. He was only moments away from the poisonous soil and certain death when he twisted, reached, and vanished into ayn tarasanby idwngev.

***

Cali blinked.

She was on her own two feet, Bren's hands on her arms to steady her, his eyes studying her face. She suddenly realized that she was gasping for breath, her heart racing. Part of her wondered which had caused the greater reaction, the kiss or what it had done.

"What was that?" She managed to pant out the words between deep drags of air.

It was Bren's turn to look startled. "It worked."

"If you mean did I see *Hailneri* and your escape, then, yes it worked." Cali's breathless voice still managed to be sharp. "And again I ask, what was that?"

"The *Hailneri* can exchange memories, images, through physical contact. The greater the emotion with the contact, the more complete the exchange, which is why I needed to surprise you." Bren's eyes narrowed. "How much did you see?" Cali could hear the pain behind the ice in his words.

"Enough." Her tone softened and she gently laid a hand on his arm. "I am truly sorry about your family."

Bren swallowed hard and looked away.

"And when did your English get so good? I thought you couldn't find the words to tell me your story." Cali changed the subject, understanding that the loss was too near for Bren.

The corner of Bren's mouth twitched upward and he turned back. "It did not. You are not speaking English. It seems that my kiss allowed me to share more than that one memory."

Cali half-scowled. "Don't let it go to your head." Briefly, she wondered what the literal translation of the English idiom would be in *Hailneri*. Then she remembered the looming departure and brought her thoughts back around. "The guards, do you think they are the ones the President called about?"

Bren nodded, all humor vanishing and being replaced by something colder. "*Dazead*, the captain of *Vnaspet*'s personal guards." He indicated the bandages on his chest. "Her reputation for cruelty and her skill with a whip is well-deserved. She would not go anywhere without her little brother *Davannid*. Most likely, the other two are *Charolwg* and *Gwahts*. They are as ruthless as their leader though not quite as polished. *Vnaspet* doesn't just want me dead, he wants me broken, displayed to *Hailneri* to show that none can stand against him. He will have sent those four to retrieve me by any means necessary." Bren released Cali's arms as if he hadn't realized that he'd still been holding on to her. "I have put your entire world in danger. I must leave."

Cali grabbed Bren's wrist. "No."

Bren looked down at Cali, his expression a mixture of surprise and gratefulness. His voice was surprisingly gentle. "You cannot fight this battle and win."

"I wasn't asking for your permission." Cali kept her tone

mild. "Where would you go? You are too injured to travel in the spaces between, and you know nothing of this world. I will not abandon you to those monsters."

Bren laid his hand on top of Cali's, a puzzled expression on his face. "Why are you willing to risk so much for someone you know so little?"

"Because it's the right thing to do." Cali took a step back and drew in a deep breath. Her skin tingled where it had touched Bren's. She forced herself to focus on the immediate problem and shoved her reaction to the back of her mind. "We need a plan."

***

Cali ignored the knowing leer on the agent's face as they allowed her and her 'cousin' to pass. She knew that no one would believe that the handsome young man who'd accompanied her in from her self-inflicted isolation was her cousin, but she'd hoped that they'd be petty enough to make a completely off-base assumption. Once their minds were headed in the wrong direction, Bren's true identity would be safe. In a large black hoodie that had once belonged to Jaycee's older brother and a pair of black sunglasses, Bren fit the description of someone who didn't want his identity known, but his movie-star good looks hinted at celebrity rather than otherworldly. Sometimes, hiding in plain sight with simple misdirection worked better than elaborate disguises and subterfuge.

"Ms. Marks," President Morgan stepped forward with outstretched hand. He shot a disapproving look at Bren. "I didn't realize that you were bringing a… friend."

Cali allowed the implication to stand. "I was on vacation when you called me. I thought it only fair to bring my," she hesitated to add validity to what the others thought, "cousin with me rather than leaving him all alone for who knows how long."

President Morgan gave Cali a smile that managed to be both patronizing and chauvinistic at the same time. "He is quite welcome, but will, of course, need to remain out here while you meet our guests."

"Of course." Cali could almost taste the sugary sweetness of her response and just barely refrained from gagging. She glanced back at Bren and nodded once. He returned the gesture and reached out his hand. They'd known that the President wouldn't let a stranger near the visitors and Bren's cover would be blown if any of the guards saw him. However, based on Bren's shared memories and Cali's newfound affinity for the *Hailneri* language, Bren told Cali that there was a better solution. Cali took Bren's hand, lightly squeezing it as he'd instructed, concentrating on the earlier experience. Heat rushed through her and she felt Bren's fingers twitch. He'd told her that they could share senses, that he could hear what she heard, see what she saw, but the connection was apparently stronger than he'd anticipated.

"I assure you, Ms. Marks, your cousin is safe out here." The head of the secret service stressed the word *cousin* more than necessary, the smirk playing on his lips telling everyone what he really thought.

"I'll hold you to that." Cali's smile was as chilled as her words. She released Bren's hand and turned towards the president. As she followed the president forward, she sensed, rather than saw, Bren find an unobtrusive spot to stand. She could feel him in head, observing everything as she walked through a set of double doors, down a corridor and into a conference room.

The *Hailneri* guards were standing, arms crossed, wings held slightly away from the body in a way that Bren identified as the 'at attention' position. Even if Cali hadn't known their true purpose, she would have believed their intentions to be less than honorable. As her gaze moved to each one, Bren supplied her with a name.

Gwahts. A short, stocky female with golden wings to match her hair and duel-colored eyes of brown and green. She watched Cali with general disinterest and boredom.

Charolwg. A tall, muscular male with bright red hair and orange wings. His gray and black gaze had a lascivious quality that reminded Cali strongly of her former fiancée.

Davannid. Even Cali could tell that the gangly young man was inexperienced. His hair was a shocking white-blond, his wings silver. His blue and gray eyes darted from place to place, never stopping to rest.

Dazead. Cali could barely maintain her feigned expression of surprise when Bren recognized the captain. Easily six feet tall, with black hair and wings, Dazead was the very image of an angel of death. Her green and blue gaze was blank, too blank to be real.

"Ms. Marks, these are our visitors." President Morgan stepped to one side, holding a hand towards Cali in a gesture that seemed like he was presenting her to the aliens.

Let them speak first. Bren cautioned Cali in her head. He reminded her. *Once they do, you can reply in Hailneri and tell them that you are one gifted with language. It's not common among the planets we've visited, but it has happened enough that they will not be suspicious.*

Cali took a step forward even though everything in her was screaming to run. And it wasn't Bren's influence. She could feel the malevolence oozing from the visitors. She forced a smile, hoping it didn't appear as false as it felt.

Dazead's voice was as cold as her expression. "Child, will you be able to speak for us?"

Cali ignored the reference to her age. Most people thought she was much younger than her actual age. Taking umbrage for something so small was pointless. She replied in flawless *Hailneri.* "Yes. I was brought to you because I am one gifted with language."

The three guards behind Dazead exchanged surprised looks, but the captain's eyes never left Cali's face.

"How did you do that?" The president stammered.

Cali answered in English without looking away from Dazead. "I have a gift for languages."

"Uh-huh." For one brief second, Cali thought that President Morgan would make the connection between the visitors and the stranger in the lobby. She tensed, but the moment passed and the president remained silent.

Dazead spoke with the practiced ease of one who was used to being believed. "My companions and I have come to your world in pursuit of a dangerous criminal. Bren Yev Tuar is a murderer and was sentenced to death. He managed to escape, killing several guards in the process. We tracked him to this planet."

Cali repeated Dazead's claims to the president, struggling against Bren's anger at the lies.

"Of course we'll help."

Cali finally turned away from Dazead. "Mr. President, how do we know that what she's saying is true?" President Morgan appeared confused. "Innocent until proven guilty, right? That's the American way."

"But they're not American." President Morgan glanced nervously at Dazead before quickly looking away.

"We help refugees, we don't give them back to tyrants they ran from. No matter where they're from." Cali felt Bren's surprise at the steel in her voice.

"I don't know." The president's voice wavered. "You saw all of those people outside. Most of them are viewing our visitors as some sort of supernatural sign. Angels, if you will. How am I supposed to tell them that their angels are lying?"

"They're not angels, Mr. President." Cali fought to keep her frustration at bay. "They're aliens. And they're hunting another of their kind. You can't allow public opinion, especially one based on wrong information, be the basis for your actions."

"Has our quarry been spotted?" Dazead interrupted. When Cali didn't respond immediately, the captain's polite façade cracked. "If you have found Bren Yev Tuar, you must turn him over to us."

Cali's own temper flared at the insolence. "On whose command?"

"The king of *Hailneri*, King Vnaspet, has ordered the return of his cousin."

"His cousin?" Cali echoed the words in *Hailneri*, knowing that the captain hadn't intended to include familial connection, and then repeated the revelation in English. "The supposed criminal is the king's cousin."

Dazead's mouth flattened into a thin line. "Yes. Bren Yev Tuar is the paternal cousin to King Vnaspet. If it matters, the original charge of murder is for the royal family."

Cali took a step back, Bren's fury overwhelming her. She bent over, hands on her knees, unable to speak.

"Ms. Marks?" President Morgan put a hand on her shoulder.

Dazead's eyes narrowed and she moved closer, suspicion radiating from her in waves. "I do not believe that you, child, are what you claim."

"I don't know what you mean." Cali straightened, voice still breathless.

"Yes, you do." Dazead uncrossed her arms, wings flaring slightly as she continued to walk towards Cali. "You are not one with a gift for language. You have made contact with the traitor. It is through him that you speak."

"Traitor? Don't you mean prince? Rightful king?" Cali threw away all pretense, lifting her chin and meeting Dazead's angry gaze.

President Morgan's eyes darted back and forth between Cali and Dazead. He couldn't understand the words, but the menace in the captain's tone and stature was all too clear. Two Secret Service agents moved in, shielding the president as he slowly backed away. Neither Cali nor Dazead paid any attention to the retreat. A moment passed and they heard a door shut. Cali was alone with the four *Hailneri*.

"Where is Bren Yev Tuar?" Dazead spat the words as she reached for her side.

Cali saw the glitter of black and silver out of the corner of her eye as Dazead uncoiled her whip. It cracked the air with a sound like broken glass. Cali felt a surge of anger as she realized what had caused the wounds on Bren's chest.

"I will ask once more," Dazead stopped walking, leaving herself enough room to use her weapon. "And then we shall see what it takes to make one of you talk. Where is Bren Yev Tuar?"

"Here, Dazead." Bren's voice came from behind Cali. "I am here." The *Hailneri* stepped up to Cali's side. He'd removed the hoodie and sunglasses, his uninjured wing stretching out to brush against Cali's arm. Even wearing only a pair of borrowed jeans, Bren radiated nobility and strength. If Cali had doubted his claim to the throne before, one look at Bren would have changed her mind.

"Greetings, Bren." Dazead dismissed Cali and turned her attention to Bren. "We have some unfinished business."

"True." Bren didn't flinch as Dazead flicked her whip forward, the tip grazing the prince's cheek, leaving a thin red line.

Dazead smiled, her formerly empty eyes filling with a dangerous heat. She drew her arm back with a fluid, practiced motion and then snapped it forward.

The full force of the blow struck Cali as she stepped in front of Bren. Dazead had been aiming for the bandages on Bren's chest and had caught Cali across the face, splitting the skin from temple to jaw.

"Interesting." Dazead sounded anything but intrigued. "Step aside, child. This is none of your concern.

Cali looked up at Dazead, ignoring the blood streaming down her face, soaking into her shirt.

"Cali!" Bren grabbed Cali's shoulder and tried to turn her towards him. She resisted, putting her hand on his without looking away from Dazead.

"Out of my way." Dazead brandished the whip but didn't actually use it. She repeated. "This is no concern of yours."

"Go home, Dazead." Cali kept her voice even and hard. "Return to your usurper king and tell him that Bren is under the protection of the human race. Vnaspet has no authority here." Cali shifted slightly and Bren released her shoulder, taking a half step backwards. Cali bent her right arm behind her, fidgeting with the end of her braid as she spoke.

"Mind your tongue, human, lest you lose it." Dazead spread both of her wings to her full twenty-foot wingspan. "I will consider you an enemy if you do not move. And you do not want me for your enemy."

Cali shrugged, dropping her right hand down by her side. "I think I'll take my chances." The throw was finished before Cali could second-guess herself. All she could do was watch the slender steel blade tumble through the air once, twice, three times before burying itself in Dazead's shoulder.

The whip fell from Dazead's hand as she stared at the dagger. She took a step forward, opening her mouth to speak, and stumbled. Davannid rushed forward, grabbing his sister under one arm as she legs gave out. The other two guards were just a step behind, but had no weapons, something Cali had been counting on. Bren had told her that Dazead would never relinquish her whip, but the other guards would follow the protocol required by the leader of the new world.

"What have you done?" Davannid sounded as young as he looked and Cali had a momentary stab of guilt. Then she remembered what she'd seen through Bren's eyes and pushed aside her remorse.

"The metal that the blade is made from is poison to us." Bren held up his left hand. The palm was burned black, the edge had started to pinken as it healed.

"We figured if it did that when Bren only picked it up, that stabbing you with it might be a little more effective." Cali slipped her jacket from her arms and tossed it to Gwahts. It was already ruined from her own blood. "Cover your hand with that and you can pull the dagger out. Dazead might survive if you get her home."

"Vnaspet will not stand for this." Charolwg growled as

Gwahts knelt next to her captain.

Dazead whimpered as the knife slid from her shoulder.

"I guess we'll see." Cali could feel her hands starting to tremble as the shock of what she'd done began to register. She pushed, knowing the *Hailneri* needed to return to their world before she broke down. "But tell Vnaspet that Earth is off limits. He sends anyone else after Bren and the next blade will be in the heart."

"Gwahts, Charolwg," Davannid pleaded with his companions. "Dazead needs to be healed."

Without another word, Charolwg turned towards the other three and spread his wings so that the others were nearly covered. A slight twist. A loud pop. And the four vanished into the spaces between.

The doors behind Bren and Cali slammed open and a dozen Secret Service rushed in, guns drawn.

"What happened?" One agent crossed to the puddle of blue blood and nudged at the dagger with the toe of one shiny shoe. He glanced at Cali. "Your face. You need a doctor." He instructed the agent closest to the door to call an ambulance.

Cali opened her mouth to protest and staggered. Bren caught her, cradling her against his chest. He answered, the time he'd been in Cali's head giving him a grasp of the

English language. "Cali saved me."

"Where did they go?" The same agent started to lower his gun, the reason for his hesitation clear as he glanced back down at the knife.

"Home." Bren answered again, smoothing Cali's hair back from her face. He pressed his cheek to the top of her head, murmuring in *Hailneri*.

"And where did knife come from?" The agent motioned for the others to lower their weapons.

Cali answered this time, her voice shaky but clear. "When you date someone who is constantly under threat of assassination, you pick up a thing or two. Most people forget to search the hair."

"Uh-huh." The agent stared at Cali for a moment before turning his attention back to the blood on the ground. "Will they be back?"

Cali looked up at Bren and raised her eyebrows in question. The cut on her cheek had stopped bleeding.

"Perhaps." Bren answered. He released Cali and she took a step backwards. "Or perhaps I will return to *Hailneri*. My cousin still has my throne."

"Either way," Cali reached for Bren's hand. "You won't be alone." She smiled up at Bren. "But for now, Bren Yev

Tuar, what would you like to do?"

Bren returned the smile. "I think, Cali Marks, that I should like you to show me your world."

Cali nodded and led Bren from the room, out of the White House and into the alien sunlight to wait for the paramedics. One day soon, Cali might see the spaces between, but for now, she and Bren had a whole other world to explore.

MORE THAN YOU'LL EVER KNOW

This story was inspired by an episode of one of my favorite television shows where the main character believes that the world we've known for six seasons has all been in her head. While writing it, I realized that I wanted to explore this idea in greater detail so there is a full-length novel rattling about in my head that may have answers... or maybe not.

The view from up here is incredible and makes me feel as if everything I've been through over the past two years never happened. Then again, maybe it didn't. I'll let you be the judge.

***

Jodi hooked the cable to her belt and jumped. She swung across the gap and through the warehouse window. Most of the glass had long since been broken, so she made it through with little difficulty. A few shards caught on her shirt and knitted cap, but Jodi brushed them off without a second look. She unhooked the cable from her belt and attached it to a hook near the window.

"Jodi, you have five minutes." The voice in Jodi's earpiece sounded calm, but Jodi knew that Eli was drinking antacid like water. He would be pacing the little room where he monitored her progress through a blip on a computer screen.

"I'm on it." Jodi muttered under her breath. She moved quickly and quietly across the dark room. At the far side was a locked door. Jodi pulled a thin wire from her jacket pocket and picked the lock.

"Take this corridor to the right." Eli instructed. As Jodi acted, Eli continued guiding her. "Third door on the left. Go through to the far right door. There should be a keypad next to the door. Entrance code 0-7-3-6-2-1."

Jodi typed in the code and the light on the keypad went from red to green. She opened the door and entered the room. As her eyes adjusted to the darkness, she saw what looked like a large hospital room, separated into sections by curtains. Lights shone on whatever the white-coated doctors were working on, but the overhead lights were off, giving Jodi the advantage of shadows. She spotted a lab coat hanging on the wall and grabbed it, pulling it on over her dark clothes. She grabbed a clipboard as she passed a desk and walked towards the back of the room.

"Remember, Jodi, this agent has been in enemy custody for over two years. There's no knowing how much he's been brainwashed. Be careful." Eli warned the young woman once again.

Jodi caught glimpses of other people strapped to hospital beds and felt a pang of regret that she could do nothing to help them.

"Agent Donovan is being kept at the rear of this room. He's enclosed by moveable panels, not curtains." Eli paused and Jodi could hear him swallow. "He'll be marked as patient X-19."

Jodi stopped when she saw X-19 on the panel to her right.

"You've got two and a half minutes before his doctors come back." Eli warned.

Jodi slipped between the panels and approached the patient in the hospital bed. She didn't look at the young man's face as she began turning off the various machines attached to his body. When she'd removed everything, she grabbed the edge of the sheet covering him and pulled it up towards his face. As she did so, she glanced down into the scarred, unrecognizable face.

Pale gray eyes flickered open and widened at the sight of Jodi.

"I'm here to rescue you." Jodi whispered. "Don't speak. We're getting out of here."

"Jodi?" The voice hadn't changed.

"Danny?"

***

"Why didn't you tell me who Agent Donovan really was?" Jodi paced the width of the trailer. She knelt next to the wiry, middle-aged man who had guided her through the successful rescue.

Eli sighed. "We weren't sure if X-19 was Danny. We didn't think you'd recognize him even if it was. It was for your own safety."

"Eli, the CIA recruited me two months after Danny disappeared. Have they known where he was all this time?"

Eli shook his head. "We thought he died on a mission. We found out that there was a possibility that he was alive only a couple of weeks before we gave you this assignment. Chalker didn't even want you to have it, but I knew you'd kill me if I didn't let you do it."

Jodi glanced over where Danny lay on the floor, monitored by several government doctors. "Will he be okay?"

"I don't know." Eli answered honestly. "Jodi, I'm sorry I never told you that Danny was an agent. I wasn't allowed to. You know how that goes. Even after he disappeared, I couldn't say anything."

"That's okay." Jodi stood again. "When we get back, I'm resigning. No more secret agent. I'm going to make sure Danny gets better and we're both going to have a normal life."

"Okay." Eli nodded. As Jodi turned away, his face grew grim and he reached into the pocket of his jacket.

***

"Jodi. Jodi."

A bright light flashed in Jodi's eyes and she jerked away from it.

"Jodi? Can you hear me?"

The light pulled back and Jodi's eyes focused.

An Asian man wearing a white coat leaned over her. "Jodi, can you hear me?"

"Yes." Jodi's voice sounded rusty. She struggled to sit up. "Where am I?"

"Jodi, can you tell me your full name?"

"Am I a prisoner?" Jodi shook her head, trying to clear it. She looked around. The room was small and she seemed to be lying on the only furniture.

A smile played around the man's lips. "No."

"Can I leave?"

"Where would you go?"

"I have to get to the hospital. Danny's waiting for me to take him home." Jodi swung her legs over the edge of the bed. She realized that she was wearing a hospital gown. "Where am I?"

"Can you tell me what year it is?"

"Can you tell me what's going on?" Jodi felt herself growing angry. "Did Chalker order this because I want out?"

"Out of what?" The man crossed his arms over his chest.

"Get Chalker in here." Jodi demanded as she stood up. Her legs barely held her and she remained standing by sheer willpower.

"There is no Chalker, Jodi. No Eli. No CIA government job." The man stepped in front of her. "I'm Dr. Nations. You're in Clement Parks Mental Institution."

"What?" Jodi stared at the doctor in disbelief.

"You've been here for more than two years."

"That's impossible." Jodi shook her head.

"You were brought here after your brother Danny died in a car accident."

"Danny didn't die." Jodi glared at Dr. Nations. "I saved him." Angry tears filled her eyes.

"No, Jodi." Dr. Nations shook his head. "Your twin brother, Daniel Michael Chase died in a car accident twenty-eight months ago. You were in the car behind him and saw it all. You couldn't save him, so you retreated into your mind and created this world where you became a secret agent for the CIA. A world where you could be the hero and save people. A world where you could rescue Danny from an enemy country and everything could be all right."

"No."

As Dr. Nations moved closer, Jodi lashed out, hitting the doctor in the face. He went down, stunned. She ran for the door and wrenched it open. Her bare feet barely felt the cool tile as she ran down the hall. She could hear Dr. Nations shouting behind her. At the end of the hall, the only way to go was up the stairs, so she went.

***

I can hear them coming up the stairs behind me and I know I don't have much time. So, which is it? Have I merely dreamed the past two years of my life? Is my brother really dead? Or, is there something more behind this? Am I really crazy? I don't know. All I know is that if they catch me, I'll never know for sure. What do I do now? I step up onto the ledge and face the door. I have only moments to decide. If I have been here, in this institution this whole time, then I can get better. If not, then I'll be a prisoner here for the rest of my life. I couldn't live like that. I take a deep breath as the door opens. I make my decision.

.

THEY CAME AT NIGHT

This was one of those ideas that just grabbed me and wouldn't let go until I wrote it down. We see so many sci-fi and fantasy shows about our world being invaded, which I think is a bit strange from a country founded by 'invaders.' I wrote two stories with that concept in mind, the second of which you'll see a little later in the book.

I'm writing this down because I will not live much longer. In less than a week, I have seen my entire world destroyed. Both parents and three younger sisters shot in their backs as they ran from our home. Two older brothers murdered by the creatures that came in the night. The beasts dragged two childhood friends into the dark as we ran – I have not seen them since. I fled into the forest alone. I have been running, trying to escape, but I fear that I am the last of my race alive; if this is true, escape cannot come. I can hear them surrounding my hiding place, plotting, waiting.

Once we are gone, I believe they will claim this world as their own. Will their descendants know the truth? I doubt that these creatures will pass down the bloody heritage of how this world came to be theirs, so I will record it in hopes that someone will find it. Whatever they have told you, it is a lie, a false history to hide their crimes.

The sun comes up now. I can feel myself growing weaker and I know soon they will come for me. They know I have not had water or food in days. I must finish. I must tell the story.

They came at night, descending from the black sky in silver ships covered with strange markings. We foolishly believed they came in peace, for they appeared to emerge from their ships unarmed. We went forward to greet them, overjoyed with the prospect of meeting a new species. As soon as we drew close enough to see, one uttered a command in a harsh language I could not understand. The creatures raised their hands and we saw the weapons they had been concealing. We tried to tell them we had no weapons, that we did not wish to fight, but they did not listen. They slaughtered thousands that night; millions more since. Perhaps I am indeed the last.

I do not know why they chose my world. Perhaps it is similar to their own home, an abundance of water and oxygen. I will never know. You know now what really happened. What will your actions be? Will you accept the history they have given you? Now that your eyes are opened, will you free others similarly blinded by lies? Will you force them to acknowledge their actions?

My time has come. I can now see the aliens getting closer. One speaks, but I cannot understand the words. He seems to be the leader, motioning the others towards me, weapons in hand. I can see his strange eyes peering into the hollow at me. Only two eyes; both in the front of a smooth face. Equally strange are the markings on his clothing, which I now believe are a language. As the leader raises his weapon, I try to copy the markings before my end. NAS

THE WAY IT ENDS

Originally written for a writing contest, this is one of a handful of stories that generally causes people who know me to start giving me wary looks. Though I'm not entirely sure where this whole idea came from, rest assured that I actually have a great relationship with both of my parents. I'm not sure if that makes this less or more disturbing.

Scott Dean was a graduate student studying law at Princeton when he met my mother. She had decided to go to college after being out of school for eleven years. She'd had me just after graduating high school and, instead of marrying the drunk who had fathered me, she decided to raise me alone. She spent the next ten years working fast food and retail before deciding to go to Princeton.

Her name was Isabella Spruce and when she started college at twenty-nine, she still looked like a teenager. Thick, black curls hung almost to her waist. Luminous blue eyes in an angelic face. Though barely five feet tall, she carried herself with authority. No one who met her ever disliked her. I know that sounds impossible, but if you had met her, you'd agree.

I was barely ten years old, but I still remember when she came home that night. She had been at the school library, studying late while I stayed with a neighbor down the hall. Mom practically flew into the room, gathered me up, thanked Sarah and swept me back to our little apartment. Her face was glowing as she gushed about this amazing guy she'd met while looking for a chemistry book. "Absolutely gorgeous," were the words she used to describe classically handsome, blond-haired, brown-eyed Scott.

Scott was the only thing she talked about that night and the next day. She went out to dinner with him the weekend after they first met. She must have told him about me on that date because the second date was a family affair. We all went miniature golfing.

I saw Scott for the first time that sunny spring morning. Dimples creased his tanned face. A pleasant face. A handsome face. His sun-bleached hair was perfect, not a strand out of place. He was huge, and not just from a child's perspective. He towered over my mother; his muscular arms almost the size of her waist. He greeted me cordially enough, with that condescending attitude that most adults use with children who are generally smarter than they are. As he patted my head, a fluttering began in my stomach.

As a child, we all often get premonitions that we unthinkingly act upon because we haven't grown up enough yet to begin analyzing everything. I took an instant disliking to Scott Dean and he knew it from the moment he patted my head. His eyes flashed and I saw something in them that I knew to be very wrong. It was gone as quickly as it had come, leaving behind it a vague disquiet that followed me the remainder of the day.

The day ended sooner than my mom would have liked,

but I feigned illness just to get away from Scott. As Mom shut our apartment door behind us, separating us from Scott, a wave of relief flooded over me so strongly that I staggered. Mom took this as a sure sign of sickness and made me rest the remainder of the weekend. She didn't see Scott again for two weeks while I "recovered." Once satisfied that I was no longer ill, Mom contacted Scott and they went out to a movie. They saw each other almost every day after that. He never asked if I could come again.

Over the next few weeks, Mom began acting strange. She seemed distracted all of the time. A few nights, she was late picking me up from Sarah's and when she arrived, she offered no explanation. Sarah was good-natured, joking that my mother must be in love to behave so oddly. Then, one night, she forgot to pick me up at all. At ten o'clock, Sarah began making phone calls, but she couldn't find her. Every hospital and police station in the county – nothing. Sarah tried to keep me from knowing how worried she was, but as the night passed in to early morning, I was worried enough on my own.

We heard nothing from Mom as the next two months passed. Sarah reported Mom as missing and made arrangements with Children Services (her sister was a case worker) for me to stay with her. Sarah and I both tried finding

Scott, but no one knew where he was either. Then, early Saturday morning, almost nine weeks later, Sarah answered a knock at the door. A thin, dirt-covered figure with short cropped black curls stood in the doorway. The person looked up and Sarah's scream brought me into the living room.

My mother entered the apartment with a stagger. As she came towards me, I backed away. She was covered with blood, some dried, some fresh; behind her was Scott. In contrast to my mother's utter filth, Scott was as neat as he'd ever been. He wore a tight smile as he shoved his way into the apartment. Sarah screamed at him, wanting to know what he'd done to my mother. I couldn't say anything. He didn't even acknowledge Sarah's presence.

He stood to one side of my mother and told her, in a chillingly soft voice, that I was the last one. He placed a knife in her waiting hand and stepped back to grab Sarah as she tried to rush to me. My mother stepped towards me, her eyes blankly staring straight at me as if she had never seen me before. I found my legs again and backed further away from her, never taking my eyes off the knife's blood-covered blade. I couldn't scream, could barely speak. I managed a whisper. "Mommy?"

She stopped, inches from where I had backed into the

wall. She looked back at Scott, questioningly. He barked at her to continue. When she looked back at me, I could see the struggle in her face. Scott shouted for her to kill me and she raised the knife. Sarah screamed at her to stop, for someone to help, and Scott hit her to make her shut up. I looked up into my mother's empty eyes, tears running down my face. She started to bring the knife down and I closed my eyes.

I heard screams.

When I opened my eyes, it was all over. Sarah lay against a wall, unconscious, but alive. My mother and Scott were on the floor, a pool of mixed blood soaking into the shag carpeting. My legs gave out and I slid down the wall. I sat there as years ticked by in the guise of minutes. In real time, the cops and paramedics burst in just a few minutes later. They didn't even see me at first. It was only after the paramedics had taken Sarah, Mom and Scott to the hospital and the police were marking off the apartment that I was discovered.

I didn't see my mother at the hospital. No one would let me in because they were afraid she would hurt me. Everyone tried to hide it from me, but I managed to hear enough to find out where she'd been those two months. She'd killed almost a dozen people in various states. Her fingerprints were all over the crime scenes and she'd written the same message with her own blood at every scene: "This is how it ends." The police were waiting outside her room to arrest her as soon as the doctors said she was better. She was severely dehydrated, starved and beaten. She had several fractured ribs and numerous bruises and cuts – all, the police assumed, from previous crimes or this last one.

When Sarah recovered consciousness, she and I tried explaining to the doctors, the police, anyone who would listen, about Scott. The police hadn't found his prints at any of the crime scenes. He claimed he'd come into the apartment to help after hearing me scream and my mother had attacked him. Sarah and I tried telling people that Scott had instigated the attack. Sarah vehemently defended Mom, saying that she had turned from me and gone after Scott, but no one listened.

Scott left the hospital after two weeks; the police took Mom into custody a few days later. She pled guilty and was sentenced to spend the rest of her life in prison. No one had believed Sarah and I's claim that Scott had brainwashed my mother, including Mom. A few weeks ago, after Mom's first full year in jail, she made a startling confession. She said that Scott Dean had not only brainwashed her into killing all of those people, but that he'd done it before. She named names.

Names that Scott had bragged about. Names of people who were on death row, who were in prison with life terms. Only a few days after making her statement, she received a visit from someone claiming to be her brother. Two hours later she was dead. Somehow she'd gotten hold of a knife and slit her throat.

Mom didn't have a brother.

STILL FREE

This story started off as being one written for a contest and ended up being published by a now-closed literary magazine. It's one of the only pieces I've ever written where the narrator is a man. Not surprisingly, the idea for this came about from watching television and seeing the plethora of commercials advising people to talk to their doctors about being put on one type of drug or another.

There were five more of them, which was two more than I'd been expecting. For once, I would be able to do only my own job rather than the extra three I'd become accustomed to handling. A total of ten workers was probably a record in this part of the country where everyone suffered from something. Life has always been different for those of us who don't suffer from any disease or disorder. We're expected to carry the workload of the rest of the world from the moment we decide not to become one of the D&D – diseased and disordered.

As I showed the way into the tech building where we would begin our fourteen hour workday, I thought back to when it all began. Well, I'm not quite old enough to remember back that far, but I'd heard about the D&D uprising from my parents, both D&Ds. Mom suffers from one of those SA (social anxiety for those not familiar with the system) disorders but I'm not sure which one. Of course, it's not enough to keep her from taking numerous trips to Europe, but it was bad enough for her to receive the disability she needed to enjoy life to the fullest. Dad endures chronic pain from ARD, condemning him to a life of pill-taking before eating spicy and acid-causing foods.

As the turn of the millennium began, society began to realize the growing problem of diseases and disorders. Dozens turned to hundreds turned to thousands turned to millions, until an entire planet was infected with newly diagnosed problems. Doctors and psychiatrists became obsolete as symptoms infiltrated common knowledge. In the mid-2030s, self-diagnosis was legalized and disability claims skyrocketed.

As the numbers of D&D grew, governments ceased to function, societies crumbled. A handful of people in various communities decided that they'd had enough of the D&D and refused to self-diagnosis. They rebelled by working, by rebuilding what had been lost. By the time I was born, the number of anti-D&D had grown and were now relied upon to perform the work to keep the D&D from destroying the world.

"When did you refuse to do it?" One of the workers fell into step beside me. She was younger than me by more than a few years but among the anti-D&D, age doesn't really matter. I smiled at her, hoping I could ask her out after work.

"When I was twelve." I opened the main door and held it for her. "You?"

"Last month, actually." My surprise must have registered on my face because she blushed and continued. "I know, it's weird for anyone to decide to be anti-D&D once they're an adult, but I really was sick growing up."

"Oh." I shrugged. Typical excuse of a rebellious D&D. She'd probably go back after a few more weeks of work.

"I had cancer."

My eyebrows raised. When D&D rose to power, serious problems didn't get as much attention from the medical community. Cancer and AIDS research gave way to pastel pills and disability income. Most people who had real physical issues didn't make it long enough to decide if they wanted to be D&D or not. I'd never met someone who had been sick for real. "How'd you..."

"My father. He's a doctor and he made a hospital give me treatment." She slid into the terminal next to mine.

"Must have been nice growing up in an anti-D&D family." I knew I had a trace of jealousy in my voice, but that was only to be expected. All three of my siblings were D&D. My family hadn't spoken to me since the day I refused to self-diagnosis. I'd met up with some other anti-D&D people and moved to the community house where others like me find a home. Now, I was the leader of the house and that's why I got the tech building instead of one of the road or cleanup crews.

"My mother is D&D and so's my little brother."

"Sorry."

"She's SWWMS; he's ADHDBC."

It's funny how a once-intelligent society now sounds like alphabet soup. I choked back the chuckle at the thought and instructed my crew on their duties. The first anti-D&D group had managed to get the computers up and running before they died off and the next two generations hooked up as much as possible to the big city mainframes. That means my crew of ten can do the work of a hundred with the help of various robots and machines. Our main jobs are to keep the lights on, the water clean and the food processing plants running.

"Does it get easier?" She gave me a sideways look when she asked the question. Her voice was nonchalant but that look said more than words or tone ever could.

"Being different? Being a freak?"

She nodded.

I thought about it for a minute. If I told her the truth, that not being one of the D&D, not being sick, meant that the world would forever see you as an outsider, that your family would probably deny your existence, that eventually the work would wear your body out years before its time... I didn't know if she could handle it.

"Tell me the truth."

"No. It doesn't. If you're not D&D, you're not a person.

You're not real, at least not to anyone outside our community. We do all the work and get none of the credit. We fend for ourselves and usually die young."

"Then why?" She faced me.

She was so young. So innocent. I wish I could remember what it's like to be like that.

"Because we're free. We're not slaves to symptoms and petty annoyances that everyone else doesn't know how to just deal with." I smiled, hoping that the words would give her something. "We're free."

Six months later, while trying to fix a broken machine, she died – still free.

THE TUEUR CHRONICLES

This five-part series has been around the block and back again. Originally intend to be published by an online magazine, the ezine closed before the stories could be released. The first two parts were later published by Lite Publishing as e-books and are reprinted here with their permission. I personally released the final three parts on Amazon in e-book form. This is the only place where all five parts can be read together.

The Tueur Chronicles
Part 1.1: Kairell – The Guardian

Before time began, one of the Ancient Ones rebelled against the Creator, beginning the cycle of evil that would infect every world the Creator designed. Knowing that his creations could not stand against Evil and survive, the Creator bestowed gifts, some small, some powerful. Among those chosen to receive these gifts, the most powerful would lead whoever chose to follow. Each world had their own name for the Creator, for Evil and for their champion. Most often, though, the one who would stand against Evil was called the Tueur.

****

The screams still echoed in Tinoa L-Anyika's ears even though they had been silenced for a full day. Every weary step sent a painful jolt through her body and every time she closed her eyes, she saw the brilliant orange flames engulfing her village and smelled the sickening stench of burnt flesh. These memories failed to fade into oblivion as the hours passed. Instead, she found her mind taken back to the edge of the village, unable to stop herself from walking forward, unable to stop what she knew she would see with gruesome clarity, reliving each horror.

She'd been on a forced march since then and, as the sun began its descent into the western sky, her captors showed no signs of stopping. Tinoa didn't mind the torturous pace they set, knowing that she wouldn't be able to sleep for a long while, no matter how exhausted her body became. Every time she closed her eyes, she would see, hear and smell the past. And so, she stumbled on through the woods, driven along by silent soldiers and lost in the grisly mental replay of the previous day.

****

At seventeen, Tinoa was the eldest daughter in the poorest family of Hemry. Because her two older brothers, Lubec and Gaheris, were occupied with their various soldier duties, Tinoa's parents often gave her the responsibility of caring for the six younger brothers and sisters. The next oldest under her was only thirteen, and the youngest barely two years old, leaving Tinoa with little time for anything outside of her siblings. Very rarely, but often enough to make life pleasant, Tinoa's mother, Kai, would stay home from the fields to allow Tinoa a few precious hours to herself. She'd made such a promise the night before and Tinoa had gone to sleep as early as she could in preparation.

As the sun began its ascent into the eastern sky, Tinoa rose early, so as not to miss a moment of her promised freedom. Tinoa had the morning to herself, but at noon, she would return home so her mother could go to the fields with the midday meal for the extended family she worked alongside. It wasn't much time, but Tinoa intended to enjoy it all. She washed quickly, tying back her hair in a simple braid, and donning a comfortable pair of pants and a worn tunic. Almost as an afterthought, she slipped a small dagger into her waistband at the small of her back.

Before any of her numerous siblings could beg Tinoa to take them with her, she slipped out the back door and headed towards Nodowen, the closest of the mountains that sheltered Hemry in its verdant valley.

The people of Hemry often joked that Tinoa was a *Vira*, a

word of the ancient tongue used throughout mythology.
Roughly translated, it meant someone who based most of their
actions on either visions or strong intuitions. For Tinoa, it had
always been the latter. As long as she could remember, she'd
made decisions based on these intuitions and never regretted
it. That morning, though she had originally intended to use
her free time to visit a lifelong friend Cassiel Chu-ker, the
feeling in her soul pulled her towards Nodowen. Although she
had not seen Cassiel in almost two weeks, she had never
ignored one of her feelings before and didn't intend to begin
now. She allowed her feet to follow the direction her heart
bade her to go.

By midmorning, Tinoa reached the foot of the mountain.
The sun burned brightly and promised to only get hotter as the
day progressed. It was nearing the end of the hot season but
there was still time for a few more sweltering days. Tinoa's
freckled skin had already reddened under the glare, her hair
shining like fire as her braid swung near her waist. She
continued up Nodowen, following an ancient path worn down
by the feet of ancestors long forgotten. As she reached the

point where she knew she must turn back or return late, she stopped at a stream. The cold water, straight from the glacier atop Nodowen, slacked her thirst and cooled her body. As she stood, she felt someone watching her. Her fingers twitched towards the weapon at her back.

"Show yourself, stranger." Tinoa's quiet voice held authority.

"I mean no harm." A male voice came from the forest lining the path.

Tinoa turned towards the voice as the speaker emerged from the shadows. He was a young man, probably only a few years older than Tinoa herself. He was as dark as she was fair. Black curls framed a youthful face from which dark eyes, much older than the rest of him, peered intently at Tinoa.

****

The new moon was nearly overhead as Qade made his way through the dense Ruela Forest. The Maku were arrogant enough to believe that no one would dare follow them and took little care to cover their trail. Qade had no difficulties following the destructive path through the trees; a great assistance since he was able to focus most of his attention on solving the difficult problem of how to retrieve Tinoa from her captors who outnumbered him by far too many. He only hoped that they were as equally arrogant regarding the Tueur as they were in most other areas and that they would have wanted to return to their base as quickly as possible, leaving Tinoa's feet unbound. If they had tied and carried her, the rescue would prove to be quite difficult since he would be forced to fight the Maku rather than distracting them while she ran.

As he started to form his plan, Qade found himself distracted by the memory of his first sight of Tinoa. Though it had happened just the day before, it felt as if a dozen years had already passed.

****

"Tinoa L-Anyika?" Qade forced his voice to be steady as a shock of excitement raced through his body. This was the one, he could feel it in his very soul. His entire being hummed with anticipation.

The young woman nodded. While her stance appeared relaxed, Qade could see that every muscle was tensed for battle if he proved to be an enemy. Her pale gray eyes never left Qade's face. She was younger than he had originally thought; probably at least three years younger than his own twenty, if not younger. He took a deep breath and spoke in a surprisingly steady voice considering how badly his hands were shaking. "I am Qade Am-Gould." Qade held up his hands, palms up so she could see that he bore no weapons. He was thankful to see that he had been able to stop the trembling before the girl had seen it. He took a step forward. "I have come from Efas on behalf of the Assembly to declare your Calling, and to bring you back to them so you might begin your training."

The girl laughed, a light, melodious sound that danced across the mountain breeze. "I honestly say, stranger Qade, that I do not understand a word of what you speak."

Qade blinked, surprised. "You are the Tueur." At Tinoa's blank look, he clarified: "the Guardian of all Kairell."

Tinoa shook her head, an amused smile still playing about her lips. "I am just Tinoa L-Anyika of Hemry and I must return home. I have duties to my family that must be cared for." She turned to head back down the mountain, still chuckling under her breath.

Qade stared after the young woman in shock. He'd heard of Tueur who hadn't known of their calling, but they had all known of the Maku and the legends surrounding them. Therefore, they had not taken much time to accept the fact of their own role as Tueur. Many of them had already been involved in the fight against the creatures and were delighted to have new powers with which to fight the demons. He never imagined that one could be called who had no knowledge of the battle raging throughout Kairell.

He called after her. "Do you not know of the Maku? Have you not heard of the Guardian who is called to protect the people of this world?"

The young woman turned back. The half-curious look on her face told him that something within her stirred at his words, but she showed no signs of recognition. "I have no knowledge of any of these words you speak," she finally said, taking a step back towards him, curiosity evident.

"When this world was created," he began the story in a low voice, letting himself fall into the familiar rhythms of the tale. "Back before Time began, a similar world was formed for the demons who roamed the heavens. The Creator banished the demons into that separate world, but once Time began and the ways of our world came to pass, the barrier between the worlds wore thin, allowing some of these creatures access to Kairell. These demons have the appearance of Kairellians, but they never lost their true essence. When they crossed into our world, they were forced to take on physical forms to survive, but their core still remains demon. In these forms, they can breed with Kairellians, creating more of their own. They are demon-hybrids who can be killed, but not easily for their demonic nature gives them powers beyond any normal Kairellian. They are called Maku." He could feel Tinoa's eyes on him, taking in every word, no matter how skeptically. He rushed to finish before she decided to leave. "As the Maku entered Kairell, the

Creator, knowing that the Kairellians could not battle the Maku and win on their own, set a plan into motion. One was chosen; one whose heart was pure and right. This one was given the power and strength to fight the Maku. He began the cycle of the chosen. Upon the chosen's death, another man or woman is called. In the ancient tongue, he or she was known as the Tueur. The word we use now is Guardian."

"And I am this Guardian?" Qade watched Tinoa's amused smile fade into disbelief. "You believe that I am this chosen warrior?"

"Yes." He continued as a proud light coming into his eyes. "As a child, I was Fore-called to be a Companion – one who trains the Guardian and assists with their battle against the Maku, though I have none of the strength of the Tueur. I have trained since that time, waiting for my time to come. Not long ago, I was Called." Qade took a step towards Tinoa. "Now our need for the Guardian grows stronger. The Assembly has learned that the Maku have found a way to release the Source."

"The Source?" Tinoa flinched at the name.

Qade could see the bumps rise on her arms and the color drain from her face. She might not know the stories, but her insight was well-honed. "The Source is beginning of all that is evil, all that is corrupt and decadent." Qade's eyes darkened with anger. "The Source would tear down the barrier between the demon world and ours. Full demons would walk the earth in physical form – and wipe us from it. Only the Guardian can stop it."

"You must be mistaken." Tinoa's voice was barely a whisper. "I cannot be this warrior you seek. I am young, and untrained. My brothers are soldiers, perhaps you seek them."

Qade moved forward until he was close enough to touch her, keeping his hands at his sides. He looked deep into her eyes. "You are the chosen one, Tinoa L-Anyika. You are *Tueur*, Guardian of the Kairellians."

A quiet fell over the pair as time froze. Qade caught Tinoa's gaze, holding her, unable to move, barely able to breathe. He watched the release of Kairellian power wash over her, gold and green and bright, the very essence of the world the Creator had designed.

****

Tinoa could feel every inch of her skin humming the moment the stranger's words left his mouth and hung in the air. Everything around her came into sharp focus and she gasped, the air flooding her lungs more fully than it ever had before. She could taste the energy on her tongue, feel it invading every part of her body Qade slowly reached out a hand and Tinoa felt her arm lifting of its own volition, reaching towards Qade. She watched it, unable and unwilling to stop it.

Behind her, a barely muffled explosion shattered the silence and broke the moment. Tinoa spun around, her eyes and ears telling her what her heart already knew and denied. From the valley below, thick black smoke curled up into the late morning sky. A breeze blew the smoke towards the pair, and brought with it the faint sounds of battle. Tinoa started to run and was jerked back as Qade caught her arm.

"It is the Maku."

Tinoa could feel the urgency in Qade's voice, but a

sudden thought caused her to ignore it. She stared at Qade, her eyes blazing with accusation. "They followed you. You brought them here." She started to pull away, to move towards her village.

"We must leave now!" He was insistent, his grip tightening until she knew her flesh would be bruised. "While we still have time."

"My family is down there!" Tinoa yanked her arm away, ignoring the pain.

"They are already dead." Qade's words were flat, his eyes darkened to near black. She recoiled as if she'd been hit. "There is nothing you can do for them."

"If it were your family..." She began to speak.

Qade cut her off. "It was. A little over a year ago." He turned away, the pain she couldn't read on his face held in his voice. "Both parents, three sisters and two brothers." His voice wavered, but he continued with barely a pause. "A wife and unborn child. All gone. All massacred by the Maku."

Tinoa's voice was soft. "Then you understand what I have to do."

Qade looked at her, dark eyes now blazing. "If they take you, millions more will die. You cannot ignore your calling!"

Tinoa felt the truth in his words, but couldn't ignore what was in her heart. If she left her family to die, was she worthy to be what Qade had called her? How could she protect all of Kairell if she couldn't even protect her family, her home? "I have to go." Without another word, she ran down the path towards Hemry.

****

A hard yank on the rope binding her wrists sent pain shooting up her arms and forced Tinoa back to the present. As the memory faded to the back of her mind, hidden but not forgotten, Tinoa stretched her aching limbs as much as she could. She felt the muscles gratefully expand and contract as she tested the strength of the knots holding her captive. They were strong, but Tinoa suspected that she could loose them if she had time. She doubted that it mattered. She didn't know where she was or how long they had traveled. She supposed that was one reason the Maku had bound only her hands; she would have little chance of escape in a land that she did not know and with which they were intimately familiar. Another reason, she could only hope, was an arrogance she could use to her advantage.

Without wanting to, her thoughts went back to the previous day when she had reached her village. Those Qade had called Maku walked among the smoldering ruins, searching for survivors. She'd ignored her desire to flee and managed to get to her home unseen. She might have been able to escape if she had not walked to the far side of what was left of her house, hoping to find her family. What she did find had ripped a scream from deep within her, so raw, so primal, that the muscles in her neck still ached, the physical pain a mere shadow of the anguish in her heart.

She had still been screaming, unable to tear her eyes from what was left of her family, when the Maku found her. She remembered the leader hitting her repeatedly, trying to make her stop screaming, but it hadn't worked. Finally, the Maku knocked her out. She awoke to find herself being carried, slung over the shoulder of the biggest Maku, face throbbing from where they'd hit her, dried blood rivulets making her skin itch. Once the demon soldiers discovered that she was awake, the ropes binding her feet were cut and she was forced to walk. The pace they set was brutal, made no easier by her wounds or the memories that haunted her every step. After the first few hours, blisters formed on her feet and the blood started to ooze not much later. In a way, she was thankful for the distraction, the new pain in her feet giving her something to focus on other than the past.

Snapped back to the present, Tinoa straightened as the leader came towards her. Qade had been right. They did look like Kairellians. If Tinoa had seen them under normal circumstances, she would have never looked twice. Some were even what most would consider handsome. Only when provoked could any physical change be seen – their eyes turned from their normal color to a bright lemon yellow.

"Are you the Tueur?" The Maku towered above Tinoa's petite frame. He was lean but not thin; Tinoa could see the cut of his muscles on his tanned arms. He paced in a circle around her. His gaze raked over Tinoa as he walked, but he didn't look into her eyes. His features would have been attractive if not for the cruel set of his mouth, the darkness in his bright blue eyes. Dark hair had been cropped short, leaving him with little more than fuzz.

Tinoa glared straight ahead and said nothing.

"My people tell me that the Companion was near your village." The Maku didn't seem concerned by Tinoa's silence. "And something tells me that you met with him. That he told you of your calling."

Tinoa remained silent.

"Speak, child." The Maku stopped directly in front of Tinoa. She lifted her chin in the universal sign of defiance. "My orders are to deliver you alive; the quality of your health was not part of my instructions. I need only to keep you breathing; that is enough to prevent another from being called." When Tinoa still didn't speak, the Maku brought his hand across her face hard enough to rock her head back. She felt blood well up in the re-broken skin of her cheek. "Are you the Guardian?" A flicker of yellow danced across the blue expanse of his eyes.

Before Tinoa could answer, a bright light exploded in the center of the Maku camp. Her captors screamed in pain and covered their eyes. Tinoa saw a blade flash and felt the rope binding her to the Maku go slack. Strong arms wrapped around her waist and pulled her backwards into the forest. Figuring that her savior meant her less harm than the Maku, Tinoa stumbled after the shadowy figure as quickly as she could on weak legs. Behind her, she could hear the Maku recovering from the attack. The leader shouted orders in a harsh, guttural language. The demon hybrids crashed through the trees behind her, creating paths where none had previously existed. Her heart pounded as she realized how quickly the Maku would reach her. A wave of adrenaline rushed over her and she felt the pain in her body fade into the background.

The figure in front of her swerved suddenly to the right, grabbing the severed rope that hung from Tinoa's bound wrists to pull her after them. She gasped as she saw herself rushing at a boulder and squeezed her eyes closed against the impact.

****

"You can open your eyes." A familiar voice spoke moments later. "We are safe for now."

Tinoa obeyed and looked around. She was standing in a dimly lit cavern. A small opening at the top allowed enough moonlight in so she could see the person standing across from her – the person who had saved her life.

"Did you find them?" Qade took a knife from the sheath hanging on his belt and cut the last of the rope.

Tinoa nodded slightly, unable to speak. She sank to the floor, looking down at her wrists as tears slipped down her cheeks, cutting paths through the dirt and blood. The salt of her tears stung, but she didn't react. Her body and mind were nearing overload, threatening to shut down.

"I am sorry." Qade's voice was filled with genuine sympathy. He crouched next to her.

"You tried telling me, but I did not want to think..." Tinoa whispered. She flexed her fingers and winced. The numbness she'd felt was fading away, leaving her with the pain of her injuries. She looked away, took a deep breath and changed the subject. The physical was bad enough. She didn't think she had the strength to deal with any of the emotional at the moment. "What did you do back there?"

Qade sheathed his knife and sank from his crouch onto the smooth rock floor. "It was a light flame. It burns brightly for only a moment, but it renders the Maku helpless for several seconds. If exposed to too much light, their eyes can be permanently damaged. They cannot stand the light."

"Thank you." Tinoa brushed the backs of her hands across her cheeks, sucking in air as she touched her tender flesh.

"I have just one question." Qade looked into Tinoa's eyes. "The Maku asked if you were the Guardian. You began to respond just as I threw the flame. What were you going to say?"

Tinoa turned her gaze to her bloody hands. The events of the past two days flashed through her mind, each detail excruciating and revealing. The knowledge of who she was weighed heavy upon her and she knew denial was no longer an option. When she looked back up at Qade, her pale eyes burned with an otherworldly light. "I am Tinoa L-Anyika, daughter of Kai and Anton L-Anyika." She paused a moment before adding, voice ringing with an authority she'd never had before. "And I am Tueur, Guardian of the Kairellians."

Qade's smile was grim. "Then it begins."

The Tueur Chronicles

Part 1.2: Kairell – The Assembly

Branches shattered as the Maku army relentlessly marched through the forest in pursuit of their escaped prey, uncaring of what they crushed beneath their boots. Branches whipped against their skin, drawing lines of blood, but they didn't pause. Pain didn't matter, nothing mattered but finding the girl.

A few miles ahead of them, the pursued came to a silent agreement. They stopped running and turned to face their enemies. They were tired and bloody, bodies pushed to the limit, but they would not give up without a fight.

****

Qade Am-Gould handed over the weapon without hesitation. It was time to see if the girl was worthy to bear the Guardian blade. He had been tempted many times over the previous four days to give it to her, but Qade had felt that he needed to wait, the time was not yet right. She wasn't ready because she did not know it all. Until the previous night, Qade had withheld disturbing information regarding the Tueur. Now that Tinoa had the most important facts, her choice here would be vital.

He stretched out his hand towards the approaching noise and waited to see if he would live or die.

****

Tinoa L-Anyika glanced at Qade from the corner of her eye. She shifted her weight to balance herself for the oncoming battle. The heavy hilt felt at home in her hands and she flexed her fingers as energy rushed through her. Despite what Qade had told her, she stood in anticipation of the fight to come. She took a deep breath and tried to recall everything she had learned from her brothers.

She lifted the sword and readied herself. It was time to prove false the words her companion had spoke the night before.

****

Qade looked across the flickering flames at Tinoa, the light dancing across her brilliant red hair. She wasn't looking at him and he couldn't blame her. He hadn't wanted to tell her like this, but the statement hung in the air just the same, impossible for him to take back. He raked a hand through his curls, wishing there was something he could do to make amends for his words.

"No Tueur has survived two years past being called!"

Now that he'd said it, he could only wait for her response. He watched her, sure he could see tears glistening on her cheeks. She brushed the back of her hand across her face, face still turned away. Qade watched in silence as Tinoa stretched out on the ground, back to the fire, for the few hours of sleep she could get before they needed to be on their way. The Maku were gaining on them, but were still far enough behind for Tinoa and Qade to take a few hours to rest. He wasn't sure they'd have the chance again.

****

Tinoa faced the cold darkness, barely registering the warmth of the fire on her back. Her cheeks were still damp with tears but she didn't bother wiping them away. She felt a surge of anger at Qade, but it passed as she forced herself to acknowledge her own part in what had happened. She'd pushed for more and couldn't blame him that she didn't like what she'd gotten in response. Since his rescue of Tinoa, Qade had been using some of their resting time to give Tinoa more information about her role as Guardian. Still, she felt that he held back information that she needed. That night, she could hold her tongue no longer.

"What are you not telling me?" Tinoa had interrupted Qade's commentary.

His tone was carefully even. "I do not know what you mean."

Tinoa's eyes flashed. Her next words were heated. "You

have spent hours telling me about the importance of the Tueur's responsibilities, about various training and fighting techniques that I need to master and how self-control is the most important quality to have. Underneath it all is some unspoken thing. I can see you thinking about it often and your expression tells me that it is not good."

Qade looked away, but not before Tinoa saw the shadow pass over his handsome face.

"Qade, I deserve the truth! What are you keeping from me?"

Something flickered in the young man's dark eyes. A pained look crossed his face and then vanished. "I cannot say."

"You can," Tinoa scowled. She couldn't understand the mixture of pain and frustration in his eyes. "What are you afraid to tell me?"

That was when he'd blurted out the words that had turned her blood to ice. It was one think to understand that everyone must die. It was another to know that destiny had given you a much shorter expectancy than you'd thought.

****

As the Maku crashed into the clearing, Tinoa shook herself free of the past and took a deep breath. She sensed more than saw Qade do the same. The air around her crackled with energy, but she didn't stop to wonder the reason. She needed to focus on the task at hand.

The first Maku soldier broke into the clearing and stopped short, shocked at the sight of his prey patiently waiting. The following soldiers ran into the first, and Qade moved. He thrust his wrist forward and pulled his fingers back, a bolt of white energy shooting from his palm. Three Maku fell to the ground, dead before they hit the dirt.

Tinoa had a split second to be shocked before she had to act. She shoved aside her questions and, as the soldiers rushed out of the forest, she swung the sword. Sunlight danced off the blade as it sliced through the air. Moments later, it was smeared crimson with blood.

The Maku screamed.

Tinoa's blade sang.

Qade's hands flashed.

Then it was all over.

Tinoa wordlessly helped Qade drag the Maku bodies to the center of the clearing. She wiped at the sweat rolling down her cheeks and pulled away a hand streaked with blood. This time, it was not her own. She wiped it off on her already filthy tunic and watched Qade use his flint to strike a spark. Neither said anything as smoke curled up from the bodies, watching the fire hungrily consuming the corpses. The crackling of the blaze filled the silence. Not even the forest animals had returned.

"We need to go," Qade's voice reached Tinoa's ears, but she didn't respond. "Tinoa."

Tinoa felt strong fingers grasp her upper arm. She winced,

muscles already sore from swinging the heavy sword. The rush of battle had faded away, leaving her with her aches and pains. She turned her head towards him, pale gray eyes wide and wild.

"We need to go, now. If any other Maku are patrolling this area, they will see the smoke and come."

"Then why did we burn them?"

"We do not leave bodies to be eaten by animals, no matter what they are."

Tinoa nodded. Still in a half-daze, she allowed Qade to pull her after him. They crossed the clearing and plunged back into the forest.

****

"We are in Brema Wood. When we cross the Keldon River, we will be only a few days from Efas," Qade looked over at the young woman as he rotated the skinned animal over the fire. She hadn't said anything since they'd left the clearing. "We should be able to move easier now."

Tinoa's head turned and she looked at Qade, gaze haunted. "Did we ki – get them all?"

Qade nodded. "I think we did." He sat down next to Tinoa. "You have never taken a life before."

Tinoa shook her head. She rubbed her hands over her arms as if she could still feel the blood clinging to her fair skin. Qade hadn't been as covered, but his jet black hair and dusky complexion made it harder to notice as well. She'd insisted on bathing as soon as they'd stopped, uncaring that the water felt like needles of ice. Because he'd seen the horror in her eyes when she looked at him, he'd done the same, shivering as he washed away the remnants of battle.

Qade threw a branch into the fire and watched the sparks fly into the night sky. "Eighteen months ago, in Efas, I first used my powers to kill. I knew that I could not just delay the Maku, I needed to kill them or they would kill me."

"Like you did back there?"

"Yes," Qade glanced at Tinoa from the corner of his eye. Her face was still paler than normal, freckles standing out in stark contrast. He suspected he had a pallor of his own. No matter how often he used his powers, they still frightened him. "I am a *Terelik*. I can focus energy and send it in a specific direction. It does not always kill. I can stun, slow, protect or move depending on what I need."

"I thought Companions did not have powers." Tinoa's voice held accusation towards what Qade knew she felt was more deceit on his part.

"We do not have the strength and fighting ability of the Tueur – the power of Kairell – but we are chosen as Companions because of our gifts. I cannot use my powers for long periods of time. I will not be able to use them again until morning and even then, they will not last long. It takes several days for me to regain full power," Qade looked at Tinoa. Her anger had returned some of the color to her face. "The cut on your cheek is bleeding again." Cut seemed like such a small word for the jagged wound that ran from her temple to her jawline. "I can stitch it up, if you want." He reached for her face and she jerked back, away from his hand. He pulled back, immediately understanding.

After a moment, she set her jaw and nodded. "With what?"

Qade reached into one of his tunic's inner pockets, producing a small pouch. "This is going to hurt."

Tinoa shrugged. "After all of this, what is a little more pain?"

****

Tinoa made her way back to the fire, the stitches in her cheek throbbing. She'd managed to stay still as Qade ran the needle and thread through her flesh, but her stomach had rebelled the second she'd stepped away to wash her face clean. Now the smell of cooked meat made her stomach cautiously rumble, but she didn't think she could eat. She returned to her seat, determined to try. She'd need her strength. Their journey wasn't done yet. When Qade handed her a chunk of meat, she took a tentative bite and was pleased to discover that her body accepted the nourishment without protest.

"I was only six when I discovered my powers," Qade's voice was soft. Tinoa looked over at him, but he kept his attention focused on the food in his hands. "I lived in a small village just outside Efas. I was still young when I went to Efas to live with the Assembly and others like me. At times, the *Machek* can sense a Calling before the actual Choosing. Most do not know if they will be a Tueur, a Companion, or neither. A few months after I arrived in Efas the Assembly's *Machek* saw that I would eventually be a Companion. My twin joined me two years later. Hana was a *Meenek*. She could control the weather. My uncle was a member of the Assembly and he suspected that she could be a Tueur since I was called as a Companion. He was correct in one aspect. Hana received her calling six months before she died. I, however, was not chosen to be her Companion."

"Chosen?"

Qade nodded. "When a Tueur dies, the power transfers to another. The Companion for each Tueur is chosen in a similar way. When a Companion dies, the next Companion to assist the current Guardian is surrounded by – the only way to describe it is – a glow; a pale light that follows the Companion for a full day. This links the Companion to the Guardian."

"Links?" Tinoa looked up. Qade hadn't mentioned this before.

"An intuitive link connects the Tueur and the Companion. That is how I was able to recognize you as the Guardian," Qade explained.

Tinoa changed the subject, uncomfortable with the idea that she and Qade were linked in any way. "Who was your sister's Companion?"

Qade fell quiet and Tinoa did not press the matter,

embarrassed that she'd let her curiosity get the better of her. She finished her meal without another word and stood, intending to rinse her hands in the stream, more to avoid the awkward silence than any real need. Qade's voice stopped her.

"My wife."

Tinoa turned around.

"Kiley was chosen as Companion to her older brother a year before Hana became Tueur. The previous Guardian and Companion had both been killed by the Maku so Kiley and Rath were called together. Rath died two months after Kiley and I married," Qade's voice was flat. "That is when Hana was Chosen."

"When the Maku destroyed your family, you and I were called?" Tinoa walked around the fire and knelt next to Qade.

Qade swallowed hard. "Kiley," his voice trembled. Tinoa could see him fight to keep it steady. "Neither one of the girls died in the battle, but both were... I was chosen six weeks later."

"And me?" Tinoa's voice was small. She understood now why he had kept things to himself. The deaths that had triggered their own calling weren't some nameless soldiers for him. How much pain must he feel every time he looked at her?

"The morning we met."

"Your sister..." Tinoa couldn't continue.

Qade looked up, meeting Tinoa's gaze. She could see the tears burning in his eyes. "Hana was always strong. She knew that when she died, the Maku would follow the energy transfer to the new Guardian. Our *Machek* at the Assembly sensed you and sent me. Hana held on as long as she could. She knew I had to get to you before the Maku."

Tinoa reached out and gently touched Qade's shoulder. She didn't say anything; she knew there was nothing she could say.

****

Qade stomped out the remains of the fire and scattered the ashes as Tinoa buried the bones from their meal. Since his sharing the night before, neither one had spoken to the other, but the tension between them had eased. Qade still wasn't sure if Tinoa trusted him, or if he was willing to let himself trust her, but he felt that things were going to improve.

"Only a few more days. Three at the most," Qade retrieved the sword from the ground near where Tinoa had slept. He handed it to her.

Tinoa took the blade, looking from it to Qade and back again. He could read the realization in her eyes and knew that she now understood what it had meant for him to give over possession.

"Yes," Qade nodded. "It belongs to each Guardian. Hana wielded it last."

"Thank you." Tinoa fastened the belt around her waist, adjusting the sheath to hang at her side.

Qade didn't respond as he walked away. After a moment, he heard Tinoa follow.

****

Early afternoon, two days later, Tinoa and Qade reached the shores of the Keldon River. They had to travel upstream several miles before finding a safe place to cross, but it took less time than either of them had feared. Qade went in first to test the current. One he reached the point where the water swirled around his shins, he turned and motioned for Tinoa to follow. She took two steps and hesitated at the river's edge. She'd only swum in the Dyni River back home and at its most full, it had still been smaller than the Keldon.

"You can do it," his voice was unusually soft, as if he could read her fear on her face.

Tinoa forced herself to look up at Qade and not down at the river as she took those first steps into the water. She waded towards his outstretched hand and let out a small breath of relief when his fingers closed around hers.

"We should not have to swim," Qade pulled Tinoa after him.

She focused on Qade's back where her sword had been strapped to keep it from getting wet. As she followed him, Tinoa reminded herself that Qade had done this before, but the butterflies in her stomach refused to be quieted. The water rose as the pair made their way across the Keldon, each step sending another flood of anxiety through Tinoa's body. The current tugged at them, but Qade's hand kept Tinoa steady as the water reached her lower shoulders. Her heartbeat sounded loud in her ears and her breath came in short pants, her entire body threatening to freeze her right there.

"Not much further," Qade squeezed Tinoa's hand, the gesture giving her enough strength to continue.

Tinoa managed a nod. A few steps later, she noticed that the water was lower than before. She could see the darker section of cloth that had been covered moments before and she could breathe again. A few minutes later, only Tinoa's ankles were covered. Then, they were walking on dry ground and she had to fight the urge to collapse.

"Tinoa," Qade turned to face Tinoa. "My hand."

Tinoa flushed as she saw how tightly she'd been gripping Qade's hand, her embarrassment just the distraction she needed to deal with the aftermath of their journey. She released his hand and sat down to put on her shoes. The bottoms had gotten a little wet on hers since she was so much shorter than Qade, but the insides were dry. By the time she finished, her heart had slowed its pounding and her nerves had calmed.

"Efas is not far off. We should reach it before nightfall."

Tinoa could hear amusement in Qade's voice and offered a terse explanation. "I could never swim very well. The Dyni River is much smaller and I never ventured far into it. There was never a need." She stood.

"Efas is a seaport. I have spent my whole life near water,"

Qade looked into the forest.

"Thank you," she spoke softly. "Shall we go?"

Qade nodded. He stopped after only taking a few steps. He took the sword off his back and returned it to Tinoa. "No more rivers between us and Efas."

Tinoa took the sheath and strapped the belt around her waist, immediately feeling more secure with it at hand. She then followed Qade further into Brema Wood. The sun was directly overhead and they still had a ways to go.

Later, as the sun approached the horizon, Tinoa and Qade reached the top of a small hill that allowed them to see above the treetops. They paused there to catch their breath.

"Can you see the Great Kairell Sea?" Qade pointed.

Tinoa followed his finger to the glittering expanse in the distance. "Beautiful," she smiled. She felt Qade's eyes on her and felt a flush creeping up her cheeks. She hoped the fading light disguised her reaction. The last thing she needed was more awkwardness between she and Qade. Something at the corner of her vision made her turn her head.

Tendrils of smoke curled into the air.

"Qade," Tinoa barely heard her own voice. She grabbed his arm and turned him. "Look."

"Efas," Qade began to run.

Tinoa followed, dodging branches and fallen trees as she tried to keep up. Qade's legs were longer and he knew the terrain, so he reached the edge of the city first. He stood, staring in horror, as Tinoa came to his side.

The city had been burnt to the ground. Blocks of stone foundations were all that had been left standing, scorched black from the flames. From the edge of the forest where Tinoa and Qade stood, they could see the Kairell Sea, three miles away. Between it and where they were, dozens of charred remains were scattered around, unidentifiable

Eyes wide and lips flattened into a thin line, Qade began to walk, his boots crunching over still-smoking chunks of wood. He paused in front of a large pile several feet from where he'd first stopped. He knelt and put a hand over the smoldering ash.

"Yesterday afternoon or evening."

Tinoa stepped up behind him and laid a hand on his shoulder. "The Assembly?"

Qade stood and shook off her hand. "This was the Assembly." His voice shook. He motioned to a smoldering mound next to the building. A blackened hand indicated that the contents of the pile were not wood. "That is the Assembly."

Tinoa put her hand over her mouth, her stomach churning as memories of Hemry came rushing forward. The smell of burning flesh, the sting in her eyes from the smoke, the knowledge that the bones had once been people... she staggered towards the edge of the forest and was sick. She wiped her mouth with the back of her hand. As she straightened, she saw something in a small knot of fallen trees.

"Qade," she called without taking her eyes from the protruding leg.

"Tinoa, I am sorry."

Tinoa waved a hand at him. "Qade. Look."

"Qade?" A weak voice came from inside the brush.

"Lirak?" Qade began to pull the branches and trees off the body. Underneath was a man, injuries so severe that Tinoa could barely believe that he was still alive. "Lirak, what happened?"

"Water."

Tinoa grabbed the water skin from where Qade had dropped it and knelt at the man's side. She held the skin to Larik's lips. He drank greedily, coughed, blood bubbling on his lips

"Maku. Hundreds of them." Each word was as struggle, but he forced himself to tell. "On a destruction mission from Barathrum. Others joined them just before they left, with prisoners. Less than a dozen, more than five. Heard one Maku say they were a gift."

"A gift?" Tinoa wasn't sure she wanted to hear the rest. From the expression on Qade's face, he didn't want to either.

"For the Source. They were all special. Said one was from Hemry, that it was the Tueur."

Hope filled Tinoa. Someone from her village was still alive, or had been, a short time ago.

"How long ago? Can we reach them before they get to the desert?" Qade's voice shook, whether from anger or grief, Tinoa couldn't tell.

Lirak shook his head. "If they continue on a normal pace, they should reach Paradym before the moon's change. Qade, you must stop the Source, or we are all doomed."

"The Assembly?" Qade asked.

"All dead. We knew the Maku were coming. Civilians crossed Keldon three days ago, heading for Bryt. We thought we could hold them off until you got back with the Guardian. We underestimated them. The Source is near ascension. Their power is growing."

"If they are this strong, how can I stand against them? Or the Source?" Tinoa's shoulders sagged as she fully realized the responsibility on her shoulders.

Lirak looked back at Tinoa and then at Qade. "You do not stand alone. But, if you fall, we are all lost." He coughed again, the blood darker this time. His chest rose and fell. And stayed.

Qade bowed his head. When he looked back up, his cheeks were streaked with tears. "The Assembly is destroyed. We are alone. What do we do?"

Tinoa stood, the fading sunlight warming her face. She thought of all she'd learned, of all she'd seen. She remembered her family and friends, all dead. The duty she had been chosen to carry stretched out before her, promising nothing but toil and pain. And as she stood, she felt the whisper of a promise brush past her cheek on the evening breeze. She knew what she had to do. She reached out a hand to Qade. "We go after the Maku. We rescue the prisoners. And we stop the Source."

****

Qade looked up at Tinoa. He could feel strength and power emanating from her. Her pale eyes flashed in the sun's dying light and a spark of hope ignited in him. He reached up and took her hand, allowing her to pull him to his feet. "Then we go."

The Tueur Chronicles
Part 1.3: Kairell – The Gathering

The pair ran through the forest, the hunted now the hunters. Neither one had to do any tracking; the Maku never bothered covering their trails for they feared nothing. A wide path had been torn through the trees. It was this that Tinoa and Qade followed, keeping carefully hidden in the shadows. They had been after the Maku and their Kairellian prisoners for two days and had barely paused in their quest. Rest had been brief and food eaten on the run. Tinoa knew that it was only by her newfound powers that she had been able to keep moving. The child she had been just days before never would have made it this far.

Suddenly, they stopped, hearing the demon-hybrids for the first time. It sounded as if the Maku had decided to set up camp before crossing the Paradym Desert. Judging by the destruction and what Larik had told them, this Maku regiment was three times the size of the one that had attacked Hemry. Though they would only cross a few miles of desert, they would need to replenish their water supply if they and their prisoners were to survive the march. After the desert, Qade

had told Tinoa, was the Barathrum Swamp and then the Lake.

Beyond that, at the foot of the mountain of fire, was the city

of Barathrum itself. The city that bred evil. The home of the

Maku.

"Is it them?" Tinoa whispered. Qade nodded and

motioned for Tinoa to follow him. They circled around the

clearing the Maku had made. As they made their way around

the perimeter of the camp, Tinoa spotted a huddled group of

people near the center of the clearing. She pointed and Qade

nodded again. It was the prisoners. She strained her eyes,

trying to see if she recognized the one from her town, but

even her newly enhanced vision couldn't make out more than

silhouettes.

Since the sun had just begun to sink in the sky, the Maku

still wore protective guards over their eyes. They didn't take

them off until dusk settled and their sensitive eyes could bear

the light. Tinoa and Qade would have to wait a little longer to use the last of the light flames. The weapons would be useless until the eyes were unprotected.

Qade motioned for Tinoa to follow him deeper into the woods. While they had the time, they needed to rest, gather their strength. Qade found an alcove of trees and both sank gratefully to the ground. Ash they waited for the sun to set, Qade drew a rough map in the dirt, pointing out Efas, the desert, swamp and their current position.

"Why did they come down river so far instead of crossing the shortest point of desert near Efas?" Tinoa had listened to her older brothers' battle talk enough to understand some strategy.

"Three rivers of melted rock flow from the mountain of fire." Qade drew more lines in the ground. "Not even the Maku can cross them. That is why Efas remained safe for so many years." He paused and Tinoa could see the pain on his face.

"What is our battle plan?" She asked, unable to bear the

grief in Qade's eyes any longer.

Qade closed his eyes for a moment. When he opened them again, they were clear. He sat forward and began to sketch out their plan. Tinoa watched, asking questions when something seemed unclear. By the time they finished, the sun had set and the stars had started to come out. They stood, stretching out their aching muscles in silence. At Qade's nod, Tinoa drew her sword. In her other hand, she held the light flame. Qade flexed his fingers as they started forward.

They approached the Maku camp at an angle, knowing that the demon-soldiers would be guarding the wooded area behind the captors, more to prevent escape than rescue. The Maku wouldn't think that anyone would risk fighting them just to retrieve a handful of Kairellians. The easiest way to reach the captives was the most obvious – distraction and frontal assault. It would be more dangerous than Qade's rescue of Tinoa since they had no way of knowing the condition of the prisoners. Some might need help walking, taking away the option of a hasty retreat. Tinoa and Qade were both prepared to fight, though pale at the thought of what was to come. They reached the edge of the clearing without incident and paused.

Tinoa took a deep breath and threw the light flame into the center of Maku. A brilliant flash lit up the woods. The Maku screamed in pain and covered their eyes as Tinoa and Qade ran forward. As they moved, they saw the prisoners stand, some shaky, but all without assistance. Tinoa and Qade fought their way through the Maku who still hadn't regained their vision. The prisoners followed without prompting. Tinoa and Qade motioned for them to go ahead into the woods as they turned to face the recovering Maku.

The demons attacked as they realized what was happening, not waiting for orders. As Tinoa's sword sliced through the first Maku and Qade blasted the second, one of the Maku recognized them for what they were.

"Tueur!" He shouted, grabbing his own sword. He rushed

towards Tinoa, perhaps thinking of glory and riches for the capture of the Guardian. Qade killed him before he could reach Tinoa, but the damage was done. The word spread instantly. A dozen or so deserted, frightened by the embodiment of the legendary boogieman for Maku. The rest attacked with a new vengeance, fueled by greed.

Tinoa and Qade knew they wouldn't survive the attack, but they stayed their ground, prepared to fight until the end. Tinoa's arms began to tire as she relentlessly blocked attacks. A stray blade sliced into her side and blood stained her shirt, but she continued fighting. Qade's bursts of energy were shorter now and less bright as his power began to wan. The Maku were getting closer and neither Tinoa or Qade could see any way out.

"Get ready to run." A male voice came from behind Tinoa and Qade.

Neither one turned around, but they prepared themselves to follow the instruction. A bright flash flew from behind them into the Maku. At first, Qade and Tinoa thought the screams of pain came because of the light, but before they turned, they saw Maku burning as a ball of fire surrounding them.

Tinoa and Qade turned and ran into the woods, following the dark-haired young man who'd saved them. The rest of the prisoners were only a few feet away and joined with the trio as they ran. They kept up the pace as long as they could and the screams finally faded behind them. When the smallest of the prisoners stumbled, Qade called the group to a halt. He motioned for everyone to move into a thicket.

When they were far enough into the trees, Qade indicated that they could stop. Without a word, the prisoners sank to the ground. Tinoa closed her eyes and put her hands on top of her head, trying to catch her breath. The wound in her side throbbed, but the pain in her lungs demanded her immediate attention.

"Tinoa?"

A familiar voice made Tinoa open her eyes. One of the prisoners stood and stepped toward her. In the darkness of the woods, she couldn't see any of the man's features, but she didn't need to.

"Lubec?" Tinoa couldn't move.

Her brother didn't answer as he wrapped his arms around her and pulled her into a tight embrace. Tinoa began to cry as the realization sunk in; her brother was alive.

As the siblings hugged, Qade addressed the rest of the prisoners. "We need to set up a perimeter watch to be sure the Maku are not following us."

"The ones that survived are going to the north of us." A petite young woman with dusky skin and short, straight black hair spoke up.

"You are a *Machek*." Qade turned to the young man who had come back for him and Tinoa. "And you are a *Pyrak*."

The young man nodded. "I am Price De-Court of Charn." His light blue eyes were troubled. "Is she the Guardian?"

Qade nodded. "Do all of you have these... powers?"

"*Xamex*." The biggest of the group, a burly blond-haired man with sullen green eyes, spoke up. "I am Ravik Ta-Lik from Ka-Lee."

"A healer?" The first young woman looked skeptical.

"Are any of you *Kayat*?" Qade continued.

A tall, slender young woman raised a hand. "Lani Hy-Ru of Davees."

"Lani, I need you to connect these trees around us so that no one can get in," Qade instructed. "Can you do that?"

She nodded, blond curls bobbing around her heart-shaped face. She stood to do as he asked.

"*Mackek*." Qade addressed the dark-haired woman.

"Zahn A-Nyce of Anix."

"Zahn, at certain intervals, search for the Maku. Be sure they are not following us."

Anything else Qade was going to say was forgotten as Lubec cried out a denial. "No!!"

"Everyone is gone, Lubec." Tinoa repeated, tears streaming down her cheeks.

"So is the regiment." Lubec sank to his knees and covered his face with his hands. "Including Gaheris. The Maku ambushed us."

"So we are alone." Tinoa knelt next to her brother. "But we do have each other."

"What are you?" One of the prisoners, a skinny young man with unruly orange hair, asked. "Why were you spared from your people?"

Lubec looked up. "I do not know why they did not kill me."

"What are you?" Zahn repeated the question.

"Just a soldier." Lubec looked down at his hands. "They told me that I was this mystical warrior. Someone called a Tueur."

Tinoa backed away from Lubec and he looked up at her, puzzled.

"They thought you were the Guardian," Qade said. "They sensed the blood bond between you."

"Are you saying that what they said is real?" Lubec asked, standing. "That the crazy things these others have been talking about, all of this...?"

"I am the Tueur." Tinoa spoke softly, her eyes downcast.

"You?" Lubec stared at his sister in disbelief, dark gray eyes wide. "You are the great warrior that those soldiers feared?"

Tinoa said nothing.

"She is." Qade spoke up. He stepped towards the pair.

"She is my little sister." Lubec still couldn't believe it.

"And she is the chosen Guardian and a powerful *Vira*," Qade insisted. Realization dawned on his face. "You do not know of these powers, do you?"

Lubec looked at Qade questioningly.

"Lani is a *Kayat*, one who can manipulate basic elements." Qade gave an example. "Price can control fire."

A fair-skinned woman with large dark blue eyes and shoulder length brown hair spoke up. "Ilene I-Natik from Bryt. My family believes that I am a *Meenek*. I was to travel to Efas to study how to manage my abilities to control weather."

"And you?" Qade asked the last member of their party, the freckle-faced young man who had asked Lubec why he had been spared.

"Trek Ka-Lee of Kaleet. I am a *Lawti*." He glanced at Lubec. "I can communicate with animals."

"The feelings you have had since childhood." Lubec studied his sister with new eyes. "They marked you as a potential Tueur."

Tinoa nodded.

"Both the Maku and the Assembly have ways of finding those with these powers. Some become Guardians, some Companions. Some use their powers in the fight against the Maku, never becoming anything else. The Assembly wishes to train; the Maku, to destroy," Qade explained. "They were taking you all to Barathrum as an offering to the Source." He looked at Lubec. "A few times, those who track the power make mistakes. Usually, these mistakes lead to those with shared blood – siblings, parents, or children."

"They chose me because they thought I was the Guardian." Lubec said it aloud. He looked into the woods, unable to look at anyone, even his sister. "I do not belong with you. With any of you."

"Lubec," Tinoa started to speak, but her brother cut her off.

"No, little sister." He walked away from the group. "I need time alone."

"Do not go too far," Qade said.

Lubec indicated that he had heard. He vanished into the shadows, but once out of sight, his footsteps could still be heard. They stopped a few seconds later. "I will return by morning light." His voice floated out from the trees.

Tinoa started to walk after them and Qade stopped her with a hand on her shoulder. "Give him time, Tinoa. He has been a warrior for years and you are his younger sister, the one he is supposed to protect. Now he finds that you are a warrior, a far greater one than any mere Kairellian can ever be. He must come to terms with it on his own."

Reluctantly, Tinoa agreed and sat down with the group. She winced at the movement. Qade knelt at her side.

"Let me see," he instructed. Tinoa lifted the side of her shirt, exposing the raw, oozing wound across her ribcage. "Ravik," he called.

"What?" The large man came over, but didn't look pleased with being singled out.

"The Tueur is injured."

"It is not bad," Tinoa protested.

Ravik bent over her and examined the cut. "It is not deep, but the blade may have been poisoned. The Maku do that to kill enemies with the smallest wound." He knelt and placed his palms on Tinoa's side. The others watched as a soft light emanated from under his hands.

Tinoa's eyes widened as she felt the pain vanish from her side. As Ravik pulled away, she moved, feeling no pain as she did so. She looked down and saw only a thin scar across smooth, pale skin. "My gratitude." She smiled up at Ravik.

Ravik shrugged and returned to his seat at the edge of the group.

"You feel no pain?" Qade lightly touched Tinoa's arm. She shook her head. "Good. Now we must decide what to do next."

"Go home," Price said cheerily.

"I do not think any of us have anything to go home to," Zahn said.

"The Maku wiped out my entire village." Tinoa spoke softly, the memory still fresh.

"I saw them kill my family." Ravik's voice was hard.

"My home was still burning when I left." Lani's eyes

welled up with tears.

"The Maku grow stronger," Qade said. "And they will stop at nothing to bring forth the Source."

"The Source?" Ilene asked, her face whitening at the name.

"The being from which all evil draws its power," Zahn answered. She looked up at Qade, fear in her dark eyes.

"The Maku are bringing the Source to ascension. Trying to give it a physical presence on Kairell." Qade explained. "Tinoa and I are going to stop it."

"Where?" Trek asked.

"Across the desert to the Source." Qade watched as faces paled.

"You will fight it alone?" Price asked.

"There is no one else." Tinoa's voice was low.

****

Zahn was the first to wake, feeling the oncoming Maku

before they could be heard. But by the time the rest of the group was roused, it was too late. The Maku were breaking through Lani's barrier. They were evenly matched in numbers but the soldiers were fierce. They didn't seem too concerned with anyone other than Tinoa, simply tossing the others out of their way.

Tinoa reached for her sword but a hard fist to her jaw left it useless in her numbed fingers. A Maku soldier began dragging her towards the woods as the others fought against the rest. Dimly, Tinoa saw Ilene raise a hand and the area around her began to glow. Price thrust his hands forward and one of the Maku burst into flame. Tinoa saw no more as the Maku dragged her into the forest. She began to struggle and the Maku hit her again. Before everything went black, she felt the hilt of her sword slip from her fingers.

****

"Tinoa." A familiar voice woke her.

She slowly opened her eyes. A ring of faces looked down at her. Two were closer as they knelt next to her, each taking a hand.

"Tinoa," now Lubec spoke.

"What happened?" Tinoa sat up and things went fuzzy.

"Take it easy." Ravik laid a hand on Tinoa's shoulder and her vision cleared.

"A band of rouge Maku decided to get themselves back into the Source's good graces by capturing the Tueur. One grabbed you and almost got away," Qade explained. He looked over at Lubec. "Your brother saved you."

"You dropped this." Lubec motioned to the ground at Tinoa's side.

She looked down and saw her sword, the blade stained with fresh blood.

"We need to move on." Trek spoke up. "Zahn says that our friends from last night are on their way. They saw the smoke from the demons that Price lit up."

"Can you stand?" Qade asked.

Tinoa nodded and allowed Qade and Lubec to help her to her feet. "Are we going together?" She looked around the circle at the others.

"I have nowhere else to go," Zahn answered.

"Me either," Ilene said.

"We go with you. We will fight at your side." Price gave a comic bow, but his tone was serious.

"Lubec?" Tinoa turned to her brother.

"I have no powers to offer." Lubec stepped back. "What could I do?"

"You saved me," Tinoa smiled. "You have courage, and that is a great power to have."

****

Lubec looked around him. Everyone was watching, but no one's eyes held pity or contempt. They were waiting for his answer. He looked back at his sister and saw her. He saw the little sister he had teased, the child who had followed him in hero worship, the little girl who had turned into a sweet young woman. Then, he saw the warrior, the power she wielded and the strength with which she lead.

He nodded. "I will come."

Tinoa's smile widened. "Then, let us go."

Without another word, the young, inexperienced army began their journey to defeat the greatest evil Kairell had ever known.

The Tueur Chronicles
Part 1.4: Kairell – The Battle

The hot sun beat down on the desert sand. In the distance, black smoke curled into the sky. Beneath a canopy of displaced trees, a handful of Kairellians slept. They woke only after the sun was well into its western descent. As the heat began to wan, the first of the group stirred. He woke the rest and they proceeded to eat in silence. After they finished, one spoke.

"Should I return these?" Lani looked to Tinoa and Qade for direction.

Qade answered. "Some Maku might know the desert well enough to know that these trees do not belong."

Lani nodded and walked over to their shelters. She put up a hand and lightly touched the closest tree. It dissolved into sand. She continued on to the next until the group stood on a vast ocean of pure white sand without a tree in sight.

"When that food you made gets inside us, does it turn back into sand?" Ilene asked.

"Do you really want to know the answer to that?" Price grinned.

"We need to move now." Tinoa reminded them.

The others agreed and set off at a brisk pace. None of them looked at the steady stream of smoke that grew closer with each footstep. They all had heard stories about the mount of fire. Those who hadn't grown up hearing the tales had heard them all by the beginning of their third day together.

****

"The Mountain of Fire." Zahn stared across the circle at Qade. "The Source is going to come out from under Barathrum – at the foot of the most evil place in our land."

Qade's gaze didn't waver.

"What is this mountain?" Lubec asked.

All eyes turned to him.

"You have never heard any of this?" Ravik looked as surprised as the rest.

"Hemry was isolated. We did not learn much beyond our valley." Tinoa spoke up.

"Each village has their own stories about Barathrum and the Fire Mountain but Hemry did not concern itself with these tales, believing them to be only lore with no truth." Qade explained. He looked at Tinoa for confirmation.

"He is correct. Hemry did not acknowledge the presence of the Maku or anything like that." Tinoa added. "Before Qade came to me, I had never heard of the Tueur."

"Everything that comes from Barathrum is cursed, poisoned by the black smoke that pours from the mountain." Ilene spoke in a hushed voice.

"I heard that the rivers flowing from the top seep into the water and after you drink it, you go crazy because your thirst can never be quenched." Trek's voice was low.

"No one has ever lived to tell the true story of what lies across Barathrum Lake." Zahn added. "But those from my village who ventured close enough returned with reports of hideous beasts and Maku taller than trees."

"It is said that anyone who does return from the lake is never the same. That their mind is destroyed. Some evil invades their thoughts and drive them insane." Price was serious for once. The childhood tales of boogiemen had spooked all but Qade, Tinoa and Lubec. Even Ravik was nervous.

"We do not know any of this for certain." Qade broke in. "For as Zahn said, no one has ever returned from Barathrum."

"How do you know where the Source will ascend?" Ravik asked.

"Our *Machek* saw it several years ago and recorded his prophecy. We did not know when it would come to pass." Qade answered. He looked at each one. "We are Kairell's only hope."

****

Tinoa squeezed Qade's hand as she followed him into the Barathrum River. She wasn't nervous about her proximity to the center of evil. While she appreciated the reality of the Maku, unlike the others, she and Lubec hadn't grown up in constant fear of the demon world that lay so close to their own. Tinoa was more concerned with the immediate threat of crossing the river. This one was far deeper and stronger than the Keldon. The current was almost violent, a warning to those who dared cross.

Lubec glanced over at Tinoa as he reached out a hand to

steady Lani. Tinoa gave Lubec the most reassuring smile she could muster and squeezed Qade's hand tighter. She flushed when Qade looked back at her in concern, but didn't let go.

"Not much further." Qade kept his voice low. He didn't want the others knowing how scared Tinoa was. Seeing the Guardian frightened by a river crossing would not boost their morale. He didn't think they would understand that the upcoming battle was less of a fear than the water for the young woman.

Tinoa nodded, not trusting herself enough to speak. The water was already up to her shoulders and she feared it would only get deeper. She didn't know what she'd do if her feet lost contact with the rocky riverbed.

"Lani!" A scream tore through the roar of the river. Ilene stared, hand still outstretched.

Qade moved to go after the young woman.

"Qade! No!" Everyone stared at Lubec. "You have to get them to Barathrum." Lubec looked at Tinoa, their eyes meeting for a moment before he dove into the river.

"Lubec!" Tinoa screamed.

"Move!" Qade pulled Tinoa after him. "Ravik, get the girls to the other side."

Ravik grabbed Ilene's arm and began to drag her. Price and Trek each took one of Zahn's arms. The group reached the ankle deep swamp that served as a shore and turned to see if they could spot their friends.

"I do not see them." Trek looked to the others for confirmation.

Everyone else looked at Zahn. She didn't acknowledge them at first as she stared down the river. Finally, she shook her head. "Nothing. But they might be too far away for me to sense them."

"We need to follow the river." Ilene said.

Qade shook his head. "No, we must press on to Barathrum. If they are alive, we will meet with them again."

"You cannot be serious." Zahn stared at Qade. "You want to leave Lani and Lubec?"

"No, but we cannot take the time to search for them."

"Qade..." Trek started to protest but was interrupted.

"We go on. Now." Tinoa's voice was flat.

"Tinoa, your brother." Ilene began.

"I know who he is." Tinoa cut her off. Her face was pale, but her eyes dry. "But if we do not stop the Source, saving Lani and Lubec will not matter." She looked at each of her companions. In her eyes, they saw her pain, but they also saw the hard light of determination. Qade was the last. She nodded imperceptibly.

"This way." Qade began to walk. Tinoa fell in step behind him. The others had no choice but to follow or be left behind.

Their pace was slower now, as much from grief as from exhaustion. No one spoke, so the only sound was Ilene's muffled crying. None of the others allowed themselves to give in to their tears. Not even Tinoa, though her eyes burned with them. The group stopped for the day at the edge of the lake, close enough to smell the sulfur from the other side.

"How will we cross without Lani here to make the rafts?" Price broke the silence. "We cannot make a boat without supplies and we have nothing in this swamp."

Qade found the driest patch of ground available and sat down. The others followed his example. "Trek, use your gift to find anything that might be willing to carry us across."

Trek nodded and stared into the murky lake waters. The rest watched in silence, not sure what they would do if this didn't work. Finally, he shook his head. When he turned his gaze back to his companions, his eyes were troubled.

"Nothing?" Price asked.

"Nothing you want to know about." Trek's voice wavered.

"The creatures of the lake serve the Source." Qade sighed as Trek nodded. "It is as I feared."

"What now?" Ilene asked.

"We find the shortest spot to cross." Tinoa answered, her voice flat. "We will rest here and cross at midday."

"In the middle of the day?" Ravik was skeptical.

"The Maku are overly sensitive to any light. The sun at its zenith nearly blinds them, even with protective gear." Qade saw Tinoa's intentions.

"So they will not see us coming." Price smiled, but it only lasted for a moment before his face fell at the memory of their lost companions. "How could you leave them?" He looked at

Tinoa. His voice was sharp. "Your own brother!"

Everyone held their breath, unsure how the Tueur would react to the accusation. When she spoke, her voice was soft, as if she were soothing Price. "It had to be done. I could not sacrifice the world to save my brother." She met each set of eyes. "Or Lani."

"Or any of us." Ilene whispered.

Tinoa didn't answer.

****

"We cannot go any further or the water will be too hot to walk in." Qade motioned toward a stream several feet to their right. Steam rose from it despite the sweltering heat of the day. "This is the best spot."

"Then we go now." Tinoa shielded her eyes and looked up at the sun. "We only have a few minutes before the sun is low enough for the Maku to return to their patrols. Once we cross, we can rest in the long grasses until sundown."

Qade nodded his agreement and they lined up to cross the twenty feet of uncomfortably warm water. Each person took the hand of the person in front of and behind them. Qade lead the way, with Tinoa behind him, then Price, Ilene, Trek, Zahn and Ravik. They stepped into the water without a word and made their way across the river without any difficulties. They then did as Tinoa instructed and stretched out in the tall grass. Despite the extreme heat, all of them were asleep in moments. No one stirred until the moon began to show itself.

"What is our battle plan?" Zahn asked as the group prepared to move.

"They are creatures of the dark." Qade said. "We will get within striking distance of the city gates. Then we will wait until just before daybreak. If Kairell is on our side, we will catch most without eye protection and we can take advantage of their aversion to light."

"What will we fight with?" Trek asked. "None of the animals around here will join with us and we have no way of getting weapons without Lani."

"You and Ilene must counter any power they have on their side." Qade answered. "They will have people – some Maku, some Kairellians – with many of the same abilities.

You must keep their *Lawti* from using the animals against us. Ilene, you must keep the sun visible. Their *Meenek* will try to cover it up, giving the Maku the advantage of darkness."

"Should we try to free the Kairellians?" Ilene asked.

"They are with the Maku of their own will." Ravik answered.

"What Kairellian would willingly join the Maku?" Price was incredulous.

"Any who seek power." Qade spoke softly, but they all heard him. "You must fight against these as well. Do not think of them as people. If they do no recant the Maku, they are as corrupt as the demons themselves. You must destroy them if they attack."

The others nodded, not liking what Qade told them, but understanding that it needed to be done. They followed Tinoa and Qade without further questions, digesting their new information.

They stopped for the last time as the moon peaked in its orbit. They could see several Maku patrolling the gate of the city. A few female Maku stood with the guards, but the city seemed empty. And the surrounding area – field, forest and swamp – all were eerily silent.

"Everything knows that something big is going to happen." Price whispered.

"Only the soldiers are left." Qade motioned for everyone to stretch out on the ground. "The rest are probably hidden in the forest."

"Rest?" Trek asked.

"Children. Mothers who are not warriors or cannot fight. Kairellian breeders and slaves." Zahn explained. A few pairs of surprised eyes looked at her. "A friend of mine joined the Maku when we were young. A few months ago, she came back. She was gone five years. She told us that Kairellians who join with the Maku and do not have powers become slaves or breeders if there is a shortage of Maku women."

"They let her leave?" Ravik sounded skeptical.

"She ran." Zahn answered. "Her back was scarred from previous attempts. She was a favored breeder so they did not kill her."

"I do not think we need to discuss this any further." Qade

instructed. "We need to save our strength." He paused. "And I believe Zahn has told us enough." His voice was gentle.

Zahn nodded her appreciation. She brushed the back of her hand across her eyes. Price patted her shoulder awkwardly as he moved past her.

"Who is taking first watch?" Trek asked.

"I am watching." Tinoa spoke up. "I will wake everyone before first light."

"You cannot go without sleep." Price protested.

"A Tueur does not require much rest." Zahn said.

"Rest now." Tinoa ordered, her tone leaving no room for discussion. Everyone but Qade moved to obey. "You too." Tinoa looked at Qade. "We will need you at full strength."

Qade nodded and lay down behind Tinoa, feigning sleep as he watched her. Once she believed everyone slept, Tinoa's guard fell and she buried her head in her hands and wept.

****

As the first star began to fade, Tinoa roused her troops. She showed no signs of her previous emotional state. No one but Qade knew how much everything was affecting her, and he knew that it had to stay that way. She had to be strong.

"Those of you who know how to use a sword, follow directly behind Qade and I. Take the weapons of the dead."

"What is our plan?" Trek asked.

"Direct assault. There is only one way in or out." Qade pointed to the gate. "We must find the place of ascension and destroy the Maku who are trying to bring forth the Source."

"That is all?" Ilene's eyes were wide and her face pale.

"Oh," Qade spoke again. Everyone looked to him, hopeful. His tone was dry. "Try not to die."

****

Tinoa and Qade lead the way, cautiously approaching the gate to Barathrum. Tinoa held her blade in steady hands; Qade stepped forward at her side, arms outstretched. Neither showed any of their inner struggles about what was going to happen.

The outer guards were dead before they realized anyone was coming. The ones by the gate had time only to turn their heads before Tinoa's sword sliced through one and a bolt of energy from Qade disposed of the other.

Behind them, Tinoa and Qade could hear the others retrieving weapons from the dead demons. The world froze for a moment. It began again as the Maku flooded towards the gates, screaming their war cries.

White-faced troops rallied around their young commanders. They fought as the sun rose in the eastern sky. As they'd hoped, the Maku were too occupied with their intruders to notice the growing light and, as the first rays shone into their faces, the Maku realized their mistake.

"Tinoa, go now!" Qade called to the Tueur. "Stop the Ascension."

"I cannot leave you here." Tinoa countered a blow.

"Go!" Qade ordered as he scooped up a sword from the ground.

Tinoa hesitated no longer. She shoved aside the most recent attacker and ran through the gates. She heard an explosion behind her. It took all of her self-control not to turn around. Instead, she focused on her gift as *Vira*, trusting it to lead her to where she needed to go. Most Maku didn't notice the petite young woman sure-footedly running through the streets. She ran away from the garish temple at the beginning of town, heading for the far end. She didn't know where she was going, she just followed.

****

Qade gripped the sword tightly with his left hand and stretched out his right arm. As Tinoa ran past him, Qade gathered the last of his power, pulling more than he ever had before. He wouldn't be able to use his powers for quite a while, he knew, but he had to keep the Maku from noticing Tinoa. For the first time in his life, Qade drew power from Kairell itself, counting on his bond with Tinoa to help him control it. He thrust his palm forward.

****

Tinoa kicked down the door to the rickety shed. Four figures turned their heads to stare at her. They were Maku, but looked far more like demons than they did humans. A fifth figure was in the center of the group, but Tinoa could tell at a glance that the Kairellian was dead. She hesitated no longer and stepped into the room, blade swinging forward as power surged through her. Only three fought back. The other's head rolled across the floor before anyone reacted.

****

Qade heard Ravik shouting instructions to Ilene as the Companion ran his sword through a Maku charging him. Bodies of the fallen lay all around, but all of Qade's group was still alive. Trek's left arm hung useless at his side, blood dripping from a gash on his upper arm, but he was grinning as he swung his sword with his good arm. None of the others were injured; still, they were tiring and the Maku kept coming. Qade wasn't sure he or his companions could hold out much longer. He stumbled and fell to one knee.

A Maku raised his sword, his face becoming more demon-like as he smiled. His face froze in the smile that became a grimace as a sword protruded from his chest. The point disappeared and the demon slumped to the ground.

Qade's savior reached out a hand. "Come, we have work to do." A dirty and ragged – but very much alive – Lubec grinned.

****

Tinoa ducked the incoming swing and somersaulted across the ground. She pivoted on her knees and thrust the sword through the back of the last Maku. She rested only a moment before getting to her feet and running through the now deserted streets. As she reached the gates, she saw Maku fleeing into the forest, across the swamp and towards the lake.

****

Qade was the first to spot Tinoa as she cleanly sliced off the head of a Maku who had thought to take one last victim before fleeing. Qade smiled as he saw the look of weary triumph in her eyes and he knew that she'd succeeded.

****

Tinoa started to walk towards Qade but stopped all

movement as she saw two familiar faces step up beside him. She felt tears well up in her eyes and spill down her cheeks. She broke into a run. Her brother moved towards her and met her halfway. They wept without shame as they embraced, once more reunited despite believed death. The others gathered around them, tired, but still standing. Ravik began healing Trek's arm as Ilene and Lani hugged.

All relief was short-lived, however, as a giant explosion rocked them on their feet. Chunks of smoking rock slammed into the ground a few feet away. A roar, a scream, echoed from the mountain of fire.

The Tueur Chronicles
Part 1.5: Kairell – The Source

Nine sets of eyes watched in horror as the mountain belched melted rock. Chunks of burning mountainside slammed into the ground around them, but they couldn't move. They were spurred into action as a large piece of rock barely missed taking off Lani's head.

"Down!" Lubec shoved Lani to the ground and the others followed his example.

"I killed the Maku performing the ritual." Tinoa looked to Qade for answers. "The Kairellian sacrifice was already dead, but I stopped the four Maku from finishing it."

"Four?" Qade's face drained of the last of its color. "The ritual requires five. The fifth must have taken the Kairellian's blood to finish the ritual with the sacrifice."

"I thought the Kairellian was the sacrifice." Tinoa said.

Qade shook his head. "Only part of it. A willing sacrifice of demon blood is necessary to release the Source."

"And once it is released?" Zahn asked.

"When I left the Assembly, they were trying to discover a way to stop it, but..." Qade's voice trailed off.

"We have to try." Tinoa stood. "Qade, try and think of

how to stop this. I am going to find the other Maku."

"Where?" Price asked.

"I think the Source is coming out of the mountain, not Barathrum." Tinoa pointed.

"'From the mouth of hell, it will come; and with it, the fire from beneath.'" Qade muttered. Everyone looked at him. "We always thought that Barathrum was the entrance but I believe Tinoa is correct. The mountain."

Tinoa clenched the hilt of her sword in a tight fist. "Then I go to the mountain."

"I will go with you." Qade stood.

The others got to their feet. "We all follow." Lubec spoke for the group. "To the end."

Tinoa smiled grimly. "Time to get to work." She started forward. The others fell in step behind her. None of them seemed to notice the still raining debris. A piece of rock skimmed Qade's cheek, leaving a thin scratch that oozed blood. He didn't flinch. The group walked through the abandoned town, stepping around and over the fallen soldiers. They encountered no Maku as they made their way up the mountainside.

Tinoa picked up the pace, wanting to catch up to the escaped Maku. As they walked in silence, Qade fell in step with Tinoa. They moved ahead of the others who sensed their need to speak alone.

"You have thought of a way to stop the Source?" Tinoa asked, keeping her eyes on the trail the fleeing Maku had left.

"Even the Assembly had limited resources regarding the Source. We knew about the ritual of the Five and that a willing sacrifice is needed. But we had interpreted the origin of the Source incorrectly so we cannot be sure of anything. A lot of what we had was cryptic at best."

"What do you know?"

Qade began to quote. "'The greatest evil cannot be killed, cannot be destroyed, cannot be annihilated because it always is, always has been and always will be. Only the Creator is older than the Source. Kairell's chosen protector alone has the ability to serve the people through fulfillment of the ancient prophecy.'"

"What is the prophecy?"

Qade sighed in frustration. "Only the elders in the Assembly were permitted to study it. All I know is that it dealt with the greatest action ever taken by a Tueur. I never heard specifics."

"I will figure it out." Tinoa spoke with more confidence than she felt.

"And if you cannot?" Qade forced himself to ask the question.

Tinoa kept her eyes straight ahead. "That is not an option."

****

The weary Kairellian warriors reached the mountain summit as the sun reached its peak. The Maku soldier stood at the edge of the volcano's mouth, covered with crimson red Kairellian blood. As they drew near, they could hear its muttered incantations.

"With flesh, blood and bone, stolen and mine own, I call upon thee, oh Evil One, to come. Hear they servant and come." The Maku hadn't noticed, or didn't care about, the group's approach. "Thy life from blood freely mine, make myself wholly thine. Blood of life, blood of death, blood of power, blood of rest. Come now, Source of all that is death and sin and blood and hate. Come and destroy all that the Other did create."

As the Guardian reached the flatter portion of the top, Tinoa broke into a run. The Maku leaned forward to fall into the lava and Tinoa grabbed the back of his tunic, flinging him back into the brush.

"It is coming and nothing can stop it." The Maku grinned up at Tinoa and her companion. "Not even you, Tueur."

The others reached the Maku as shrieks floated from the gaping chasm. They stared at the hole, entranced.

"It knows I am here to release it." The Maku stood. He didn't care that Tinoa had the tip of her sword inches from his chest; his grin grew wider, revealing pointer teeth than any Kairellian ever had.

The nine stared in openmouthed horror as three massive creatures, dirty green as the Marta Sea, rose from the mountain. They dove at the Kairellians, mouths of jagged red teeth in velvet black pits. Tinoa swung at one while Lubec and Qade wielded their swords against another. The rest of the group thwarted the third. However, the damage was done. Just as the first creature turned, forcing Tinoa to finish her attack, the Maku dashed towards the opening and threw himself into the abyss.

The earth shook and everyone fell to the ground. They stared as thick smoke poured out of the chasm. More shrieks emanated from the pit, these far louder than those from the creatures now circling overhead. These screams promised hideous death to all who heard them.

"What now?" Zahn asked, barely audible over the cries from the volcano.

"I do not..." Qade started to say.

Tinoa interrupted with a soft voice. "I know how to stop it." She stood, placed her sword on the ground next to Qade and started to walk towards the pit. Qade leapt to his feet. The others began to rise as well, but a sharp word from Lubec stopped them. If anyone could stop Tinoa from what it looked like she was going to do, it would be Qade.

****

Qade grabbed Tinoa's arm and turned her around. "What
are you doing?"

"If a willing sacrifice is necessary to release the Source,
than the same should imprison it again." Tinoa smiled softly
and Qade knew that his look of understanding had confirmed
her decision. "It has to be blood and only my blood has
enough power. I have to do it."

Qade knew that she was right, but his grip on her arm
tightened. "No. Please, no." He pleaded.

Tinoa gently pried his fingers from her arm. "Shh." She
placed a hand on Qade's cheek, feeling the damp from his
tears. "I will be all right." She felt her own tears spill over.

"I cannot lose you too." Qade put his hand over Tinoa's.

****

Tinoa didn't speak again, not trusting her voice. She
turned to walk away. Qade grabbed her arm again, this time
pulling her to him. He held her close and kissed her, oblivious

to the chaos around them. When he released her, Tinoa
walked towards the abyss without hesitation. A strange peace
settled over her. She knew that this was as much her calling as
being a Tueur.

****

Everyone watched as Tinoa stepped up to the edge. She
looked back then, meeting each pair of eyes only for a
moment; she held Lubec's and Qade's a fraction longer. She
closed her eyes and raised her shining face to the sky. A smile
settled on her lips and she stepped forward.

As she dropped out of sight, Qade fell to his knees and
buried his head in his hands, silent sobs racking his body.
Behind him, he could hear the cries of the others, but he could
offer them no comfort.

The ground stopped shaking. The screams faded. The vile
creatures vanished. But still, the warriors didn't leave. They
knew that they had won, that the Source was again sealed in
its own world, but it had come at a high price. They stayed on
the mountaintop for hours, until the sun began to sink below

the horizon. Only then did they move.

Lubec was the first to stand. He picked up Tinoa's sword, grief written across his face. "Qade, we have to leave before the Maku deserters return."

Qade didn't move.

"He is right." Ilene stepped forward and placed a sympathetic hand on Qade's shoulder. He wearily nodded and stood.

Together, the group started down the mountain. They moved slowly, without any joy in their victory. Before they had gone more than a mile, a flash of brilliant white light blinded them. When they could see again, none could believe their eyes. There, lying on the path in front of them, was a familiar figure.

Lubec was the first to recover and he engulfed his sister in an embrace before she could say a word. The others piled on around him. Only Qade hung back.

Tinoa stood with her friends' assistance.

"What happened?" Price asked.

Tinoa held up a hand and stepped away from the others,

towards Qade. This time, she pulled him to her. After a good while, they broke apart, flushed and teary, but smiling. Tinoa then turned to face her companions. A fierce light shone in her eyes.

"I will tell you more later, but some you must know now."

"How did you..." Trek couldn't formulate the question. He gestured towards the now silent chasm and then at the ground where Tinoa had appeared.

"The Source is pure evil. It cannot hold anything that is not." Qade's eyes lit up with realization. "It did not own you and you gave yourself willingly despite the power you wield. 'And it will happen that one chosen will forfeit the power of Kairell but will not fall for nothing can hold what it does not own.' I had not thought of that passage in years."

Tinoa waved a dismissive hand. "That can be discussed later. We have much to do."

"But the Source is defeated." Lani looked puzzled.

Tinoa shook her head. "It is only delayed. A war is coming. A great war in which our world will play a part – alongside many other worlds."

"Other worlds?" Zahn asked.

"After I jumped, I saw many things. I saw the war to come, what we must do to prepare, and who will be fighting on our side. There are others like us, in worlds like and unlike ours, all who are fighting against the Source. Soon, we will all join together and fight the final battle. Now, we must prepare for what is to come."

As the army descended the mountain, Qade reached for Tinoa's hand, threading his fingers through hers. Lubec put his arm around Lani's waist and pulled her close. Price draped one arm across Zahn's shoulders and another around Ilene's. Trek put his hands in his pockets and began to whistle.

Terrible things were coming, this they knew. But, now, they were no longer alone. And, they knew that they could win.

****

"It comes." Nikko sat up straight, his dark curls wet with sweat. He hadn't had a nightmare this bad in years. Though the vision of the horrors to come had scared him, he felt an odd comfort. He murmured to himself as he settled back into his waterbed and pulled his blankets around him. "She jumped and lived. It can be defeated."

MINUS ONE

While in high school, I wrote this short story for my creative writing class. When my mother printed it out, she was so creeped out by it that she still refuses to read the novel that came about as a result of it. For those that have read Three, Two, One, *you should recognize this as being very similar to the opening scene of the novel.*

Cassidy watched in silence as a steady stream of mourners passed by the polished wooden casket, offering condolences that fell on numb ears. She fought back the intense urge to scream that she wasn't dead – it was Jessica whose remains lay in the cold, wooden box – but she knew it wouldn't do any good. No one believed her, not her parents, not even Nora. Cassidy glanced at her sister and then turned away, unable to look at the remaining mirror image they had both shared with Jessica.

She suddenly shivered despite the sweltering room. Someone had turned the heat on earlier that morning in anticipation of cool October weather, but hadn't counted on the hundreds of friends and family acting as human heaters. The cloying smell of flowers nauseated her and she struggled to keep from gagging. The hairs on her arms and the back of her neck stood up as she realized that someone was staring at her. This wasn't just someone looking at her with the sympathy felt towards one who has felt a personal loss. Cassidy could feel hatred and rage burning into the back of her neck.

Cassidy glanced behind her, catching Nora's eye. She tried to signal to her sister that something was wrong, a gesture she and Jessica had often shared without thinking.

Nora stared back, her dark eyes flashing a message that sent chills down Cassidy's spine. Nora knew the true identity of the dead Chapman girl. Nora had known all along, and Cassidy was next.

SHADOW OF TRUTH

Written for a first line contest, this is the second story that came from me wondering about seeing an alien invasion from a different perspective. This story, however, spoke to me more than the previous one and I've been toying with the idea of making it into either a novella or a full-length novel.

"So, all of it was just a lie?"

Tara stared at her best friend and ran a hand through her dark hair.

"I'm sorry you had to find out this way." Kile shifted and winced, pain written across his handsome features.

"Everything's a lie." Tara repeated.

Kile nodded. Sweat plastered his golden hair to his forehead.

"Sixty-five years ago, aliens invaded and massacred almost the entire native population. They scattered all over the planet, claiming control and setting up governments. Ten years after the invasion, the rest of the aliens, civilians this time, came. Not wanting to acknowledge what they'd done, the governments came to an agreement. They used a special group of their own people and bred them with some native prisoners with similar powers. The resulting children had unique abilities and acted as conduits for the psychics who implanted new memories into every unprotected alien mind. The Gruag ordered the remaining natives and half-breeds executed, but a few escaped and joined with other hiding natives. We know the truth and the Gruag will stop at nothing to destroy us."

"The what?"

"The Gruag. The military council of aliens who know the truth. They oversee everything on the planet. Most of the current governments don't even know of the Gruag. If they go against what the Gruag want, they are removed from power. Assassinations are all headed by the Gruag. I can't name anyone in any government who knows any of the truth."

"And you are?" Tara managed to keep her voice steady while asking the question.

"Kile O'Malley. The boy you've known for ten years." Kile struggled to sit up and the knife wound in his side oozed crimson blood. "But I am also Kile of Malrek-de. Son of Liam and Kae, the rightful rulers of Earth and protectors of the truth."

"And my people murdered your race to take over this planet?"

Kile shook his head. "Only partly. Your father is one of the half-breeds. He was going to tell you on your eighteenth birthday, but..." He didn't finish the thought as a look of pain flashed across Tara's face. "The blood of Earth flows through your veins. That is why I needed you here." Kile knew that he had little time. "The cut is deep and without your help I will die."

"I never went past Biology II." Tara protested.

"That's not how it works." Kile reached out a hand.

Tara started at the sight of his blood smeared across the palm. Then, she looked into his eyes and made a decision. She took his hand and moved closer to the couch. "What do you need to do?"

Kile relaxed as Tara's fingers closed on his. "I need to borrow your healing power."

"I don't have anything like that."

"Yes you do." Kile managed a weak smile. "It's in your blood. Earth people, my people, your people, we all have it. It overpowers the alien blood. Haven't you ever wondered why you rarely get sick? Why you look so young for your age?"

Tara shrugged. "I never really thought about it. My dad was in his early sixties and didn't..." Her voice trailed off as she realized the rest of her thought.

"We don't age as rapidly as the aliens."

"You keep calling them aliens. Does that mean that you're human and I'm... not?"

"Human is the name your mother's people call themselves. We always called ourselves *Ti-Niak*. People of the Earth in our ancient language. Now, it's easier to use 'natives' and 'aliens' to distinguish between the two groups." Kile motioned for Tara to kneel next to the couch. "This might make you a little weak." He smiled apologetically.

"Okay." Tara squelched the butterflies in her stomach. Her eyes widened as her skin began to glow a pale yellow. Kile's skin was surrounded by a light purple and the colors merged through each other over their connecting hands. Tara felt the energy flow through her and out of her fingers into Kile. As Tara's color faded to almost white, Kile's purple grew stronger until it was a deep violet.

Kile released Tara's hand and sat up, looking over at his friend as she heavily leaned against the edge of the couch. He slid to the ground next to her. The glow around them both sunk into their skin and disappeared as Tara's strength returned. Several minutes passed and she looked at Kile.

"Did it work?"

He smiled and lifted the bottom of his shirt. Though bloodstained, his skin was unbroken. "It worked."

Tara nodded once, pleased that her friend was healed. Then, she straightened and looked at him more seriously. "I have some questions."

Kile's smile softened. "I'm sure you do, but we have to get out of here. It's not safe."

"Not safe?"

"The Gruag know where I am. It's not going to take them

long to follow my trail from school to here." Kile stood and extended a hand to help Tara to her feet.

"Where will you go? Your family's here..." Tara's voice trailed off as Kile's face tightened. "What happened?"

"That's how I got hurt. They're all... gone." Kile struggled to keep his voice even. "I was late getting home last night. It saved my life. I fought with one of the Gruag and he cut me, but I managed to get away. Not before I saw the others. They're all gone."

"Kile," Tara didn't know what to say, so she wrapped her arms around her friend, feeling the loss of his family as much as she had when her own parents died three years before.

Neither spoke as they climbed into Tara's car. Kile pointed and Tara followed the direction. They traveled for hours without speaking, without needing to speak. They were bound now by grief, by knowledge and by the power Tara had given to Kile. They didn't understand what had happened in the motel room, only that it had saved Kile's life and drawn them together. Not until they crossed the border into Colorado did they stop. They both collapsed onto the beds in the hotel room and fell asleep, not waking until the sun was high in the sky the following day.

Kile emerged from the bathroom, his wet hair leaving

droplets of water on his stained shirt. He left to buy clothes as Tara climbed out of her bed. By the time she finished with her own shower, Kile had returned. She took the bag he indicated and retreated to the bathroom. Several minutes later, she rejoined Kile. He sat on the edge of the bed he'd slept in the night before. Without a word, Tara crossed the room and sat across from him on her bed. Neither one spoke for several minutes.

"What do we do next?" Tara broke the silence.

Kile looked up sharply. He wasn't sure he'd heard her correctly. "What?"

Tara leaned closer to him. "What do we do next?" She repeated her question.

"We?" A hope leapt in Kile's heart and he prayed he wasn't misunderstanding her meaning.

"We." Tara took one of his hands in hers. "We have a lot of work to do if we're going to take down the Gruag and reveal the truth. We are better together than apart."

Kile smiled and squeezed Tara's hand. "That we are." His face fell then. "But we can't take on the Gruag. My people," he corrected himself, "our people are survivors, not fighters."

Tara's face grew grim. "But I am both. I am part of each world. I've lived in the shadow of the truth my whole life, but have not seen it until now. I am a part of this from every angle, in every molecule of my being. And I will not be part of a lie."

Kile studied Tara for a moment, not responding. Finally, he nodded his head. "There are others who feel as you do. They have asked my family to lead them against the Gruag for some time. They will not act without the backing of the royal family."

"And you are the last member of that family."

Kile squeezed her hand again. "We are part of that family. Not the end of it."

Tara flushed as Kile continued.

"We'll go to them first. They'll be better organized to start this thing." Kile stood and Tara rose with him. "Then, we'll see where we're lead from there." Kile started towards the door but was pulled back by Tara.

"One quick question," she said. Her eyes glinted with laughter. "You said that the natives age slower than the aliens."

"Yeah?"

"Just how old are you?"

Kile grinned. "Somewhere between you and 'holy crap that's old.'"

Tara joined in the laughter as the pair exited the room and climbed into Tara's car, ready to fight for truth.

TOYS IN THE CLOSET

If other stories I've written have creeped some people out, rest assured that I am not immune to the heebie-jeebies. This story is actually based on a recurring nightmare that I used to have as a child. Perhaps it explains a thing or two.

The closet door creaked opened. The light cast pale illumination on the hallway walls. Shadows flickered as something crept out into the carpeted corridor. It silently moved down the hall towards the child's bedroom.

"What are you doing?" A whisper came from the shadows.

"Tremont?"

"Follow me." Tremont instructed. Amadeus followed Tremont into the deep shadows. "You heard the rules the first day you joined us."

"But..." Amadeus began to speak but was cut off.

"Since you are new, you may not understand what you almost did." Tremont patiently continued, talking over Amadeus. "It all began many years ago. I was much younger then. Barely out of the package. My fur was soft and new, my eyes undimmed by the passage of time. I didn't have knowledge of these things. None of us did. We were like all other toys, silent, unmoving, unliving. That life was all we knew until the Watcher came. He was unlike any other toy we had ever seen. He moved without mechanics, without electricity or gears. He was alive."

The Watcher waited until the boy was put to bed. When the house was silent, he sat up and looked around. He'd been kept alone for too long. His previous owner was an inventor, tinkering with his toys until he managed to create the Watcher, something much more than a toy, but much less than a human. When he realized what he'd done, the Inventor kept the Watcher locked away, alone so others couldn't be made. When the old man died, the Watcher was found and given to the old man's grandson. It was in the toy room of this grandson the Watcher now found himself.

After years of being alone, the Watcher was finally among his own. This child owned hundreds of toys of various shapes, sizes and descriptions. The Watcher climbed off his table and walked around the room, examining the others. He tried talking to them but none responded. He stopped in front of a stuffed gray elephant and stared into its unblinking black eyes.

"Speak!" He commanded, but the toy did not. Frustrated, he kicked at the elephant and knocked it over. The realization came to him suddenly. "They're all dumb. They aren't like me." He understood now why the Inventor had kept him apart from the others. He knew how to make the toys live like himself and to keep from being alone, he would do just that. The Watcher grabbed the elephant by a large ear and dragged it into the toy closet. Pale green light shone from under the crack in the door, but none were around to see it.

"I was the first of many the Watcher brought to life." Tremont gravely watched the reaction of Amadeus. "Soon, we had only to place the toys into the closet for the magic to give them life. None of us knew that the Watcher was tapping into very strong, very dark magic – magic that demanded blood in return for our lives. Our ignorance wasn't to be forgiven and only a few months after the Watcher came to us, accidents began to happen to our family. I was the only one with enough courage to speak up."

The elephant approached the Watcher with much trepidation. Many of the toys felt they owed the Watcher everything since it was he who had brought them out of the darkness, but some were beginning to suspect their life had come with a price higher than they could have imagined.

"Watcher?"

"Tremont?" The Watcher turned from the toy he was examining and faced the young elephant.

"Yes, sir. Um, some of us were wondering about something." Tremont couldn't meet the Watcher's cold eyes. He instead forced himself to look at the porcelain doll the Watcher had been looking at. "We've noticed strange things happening to our family. Bethany had a bad spill on her bike yesterday, and just the day before, she fell down the steps."

"You needn't concern yourself." The Watcher spoke coldly. "The humans aren't your concern. They don't care for us. We're playthings to them."

"When I heard those cold words and saw the rage in his eyes, I knew something evil lived in him." Tremont's eyes took on a far off look as he continued his tale. "Shortly after our conversation, the little girl of the family fell from a tree and broke her neck. The Watcher told us that the toys of hers he'd brought to life mustn't be allowed to live. They couldn't be given to another person. He said it was our duty to kill those toys. And we did.

"Foolishly, we expected that once we obeyed him, the tragedies befalling the family would cease. Not more than a few days later the accidents started again. This time, the mother. After several minor accidents, she joined her daughter."

"The Watcher killed them?" Amadeus pulled his cloak tighter around him.

"We never knew if he did it, or the magic he had called upon worked its own will. We did all agree that the Watcher had released something horrible." Tremont's voice grew sad. "When our own master began having a series of accidents, we knew it was time to act. We loved our boy more than we loved living and more than we feared the Watcher. One night, when the Watcher was asleep, we did what we knew was necessary."

Five shadows moved noiselessly across the room to where the Watcher slept. Each one had fear in their mechanical or stuffing-filled hearts, but they knew if they didn't act, their family was doomed. The elephant was the biggest of the group and it was he who carried the weapon. From behind his back, he produced a knife, the largest he had been able to steal from the kitchen. The others positioned themselves around the Watcher and waited for Tremont to give the signal. At his nod, they each grabbed one of the Watcher's limbs. He woke, but only an instant before the knife flashed and his head parted from his body. Four more flashes removed the limbs and another stroke split the torso in two.

"We scattered the pieces around the yard, burying them deep. We thought with the Watcher dead, we'd be the only living toys and as we wore out, no one would need know our terrible secret. To our horror, any toy placed into the closet now came alive. The original five who remained, decided we would never tell the others about the Watcher, but we couldn't hide our sins. Only a few days after the death of the Watcher, one of the new toys ventured out of the playroom in the daylight. We found her hours later, cold and stiff. It wasn't for some time that we figured out what'd killed her. Three more toys would die, one of the originals among them."

"What could kill a toy?" Amadeus felt Tremont trying to read the face hidden under his long black cloak. He pulled it tighter and waited for the answer.

"Only the Inventor had known about his creation. To be seen by a human when moving brought instant death. The human was able to dismiss the idea of living toys by bringing all sorts of scientific explanations into the equation, but the damage to the toy was done. Nothing could bring them back again."

"Is this why no one should leave the play room or move during the day?" Amadeus asked.

Tremont nodded. "Nearly forty years have passed since the Watcher was among us. We are now in the possession of our third family, the child's child of my child. The last three originals have died. Two were worn to pieces and buried before they could be thrown away. The last, consumed by the evil he had done, walked out of the playroom into the daylight. I found him that night."

"So you are the last of those who know the truth?"

Amadeus asked.

"Yes." Tremont stood to his full height.

"Then you're the one I need." Amadeus stood as well and drew a glittering knife from inside his cloak. "You didn't bury me deep enough." Amadeus threw off his cloak to reveal a crudely glued body. "Did you think I wouldn't return?"

"The Watcher." Tremont growled. "This time, you won't come back."

"I think it's you who won't be returning." Amadeus, the Watcher, stepped forward, knife held easily in one hand. "If you beg, perhaps I'll give you the mercy you didn't give me."

"As you showed mercy to our family, the girl's toys?" Tremont didn't back away from the flashing knife.

"Foolish toy." The Watcher spat out. "I gave you the chance to be immortal. As long as I live, the toys in the closet will live for the dark magic lives in me. You should've known this was why toys continued to come to life – the magic was not dead. It, and I, merely waited to return. Because of your shame at what happened, we can no longer venture into the light. But, once you are dead, the shame will die with you. Once again, the toys will rule." He stepped forward. Tremont stepped into the knife, surprising the Watcher as he wrapped his trunk around him and held him close, unmindful of the sharp, cold blade slicing through his cloth and stuffing.

"But I still live." Tremont whispered, pulling the Watcher into the light. "As does my shame. And your magic can not overcome it."

"Mama!" A child's scream pierced the night. "My toys!"

"You..." The Watcher managed to say as he felt his body stiffen.

Tremont didn't speak. He fell to the floor, a smile on his soft gray face as the little boy ran to the safety of his mother's arms. No one would notice the two toys. In the early hours of the morning, the others would come and bury their comrades. The child might wonder what happened to them, but would eventually forget. The closet would cease giving life and the remaining toys would wear out and die until none were left who could remember the nights the toys walked freely and the evil that brought them life.

SO IT BEGINS

These characters are based on people that I used to work with and the story itself, with a little poetic license taken, did actually happen to one of them. The Durand family was created for my fifth novel, a fantasy titled (as of this publication) The Dragon Three, *and I decided to write a humorous story about something that happened before the characters appear in the novel.*

When the Durand family went anywhere it was always a fiasco. Fourteen kids, half of them under the age of ten and most with more energy than any one person should have. Marcile Durand had her hands full. As she always did, she counted on her two oldest, fifteen and fourteen year-olds Robb and Jozy, to help. This trip to their favorite restaurant was no exception.

"Robb, make sure you keep Amber and Cheri close by. They've been running around every time we go some place public." Marcile instructed her eldest son as she handed each of the eleven year-old twins, Julie and Janet, one of the two year-old girls. Lawanda and Lacilla had just started walking and squirmed in their sisters' arms, eager to be down on their own. "And Jozy, don't let Dede and Monica cross the parking lot without holding your hands."

"Yes, Mama." Robb waited for his nine year-old sisters, Alexis and Sarah, to climb out of the magically extended interior of the family van. He then helped the six year-old twins out of their booster seats. Cheri grinned up at her

brother, quite the feat since he was already over six feet tall.

"Don't even think about it." She gave him a wide-eyed

innocent look that he knew better than to trust.

"Ouch! Mama, Dede pulled my hair!" Jozy called out

from the other side of the van.

"Man up," Robb called. "They ain't that big!" He winced

as Amber kicked him in the shins and tried to run. He scooped

her up under one arm and her twin under the other.

"*Mira!*" Jozy fell in step beside Robb. He gestured

towards his hair. His normal mohawk had one section bent to

the side. "*Mira!*" He repeated.

Robb's dark eyes sparkled. "Jozy, you need to stand up for

yourself. Can't keep letting the little ones get the best of you."

Jozy scowled, but it didn't reach his light green eyes.

"Like the girls don't have you wrapped around their little

fingers."

A snicker from in front of them said that their two

younger brothers, Jaiseyn and Henry, had heard the exchange. Robb refrained from reminding both of them that their little sisters had no problem talking all four boys into tea parties and fashion shows. No need to bring up the past. Even if it had been just three days ago.

The meal passed without any major catastrophe. As usual, Amber ended up with food in her hair, and Alexis and Sarah fought over the last piece of pizza, but as far as eating out went, the Durands counted this one a success.

"I'm going to the restroom before we leave," Jozy announced.

"Robb, go with him," Marcile instructed her son.

"Ma, he's fourteen years-old," Robb protested.

Marcile smacked him in the back of his head. "I don't care if he's fourteen or forty, you look after your little brother."

"Yes, Ma." Robb's tone was contrite.

"Now, Jozy," Marcile turned to her second oldest son. "What do you do if someone tries anything?"

"Hex him in the crackerjacks." Jozy answered promptly. It had been one of the Durand family's first rules of self-defense for years and one that they never forgot. Robb may have been big for his age with the potential to keep growing, but Jozy was a good two to three inches shorter than average. He didn't scare people as easily as his big brother.

"Very good. I'll have Jaiseyn and Henry help me take the girls out. You two come out when you're done."

"Grown boy can't even go to the bathroom by himself," Robb muttered as he walked after Jozy. While his brother went into the restroom, Robb stationed himself outside the door and tried to look interested in the pictures hanging on the walls.

"Look what I found." A loud voice boomed next to Robb's ear, carried on a wave of alcohol too strong to have been served at this particular establishment. "I found a tiny friend."

A familiar-sounding noise – something akin to a nervous squeak – made Robb turn around. A wide-eyed and uncomfortable-looking Jozy was dwarfed under the arm of a large and inebriated man.

"Robb, help." Jozy's voice was small.

At first, all Robb could do was stare, and try not to laugh. He was already going to be in so much trouble when his mom found out about this. She'd slap him upside the head for sure if she found out that he'd laughed.

"Do you have a little friend like me?" The guy blinked blearily at Robb.

"No, but I do have a little brother who looks an awful lot like your friend." Robb withdrew his wand, hoping he didn't have to use it. With a guy this drunk, there was no guarantee that any spells Robb knew would affect him much. "Why don't you let him go?"

"But he's my friend." The man's face fell. "Who's gonna keep me company?"

"Tell you what," Robb thought fast. "Let Jozy come with me, and I'll find another friend for you."

"Okay." The man took his arm from around Jozy's shoulders. "But I want another little one with funny hair. Maybe with a leprechaun. Or a goat. One of those ones that faint."

As the boys hurried away, Robb asked Jozy, "if you couldn't hex him, why didn't you just kick him or something?"

Jozy gave Robb a fearful look. "He was huge! I didn't think one kick would've made a difference."

Robb nodded. That made sense. He paused by the host's desk and quickly explained that there was a gentleman who needed escorted out. By the time the boys reached the van, their mother wasn't in any mood to hear reasons or excuses. She simply told them to get into the van and they headed for home. It wasn't until they were almost there that Robb got the idea. He would ask their father about maybe letting him and his brothers take self-defense classes, at least him and Jozy. He knew he could explain to his father everything that had happened and not risk a smack to the head. The worst Arthur

Durand would do would be to sigh. And, there was always the possibility of getting those self-defense lessons.

* * *

"*You're* going to teach us self-defense?" Robb tried to hide the disbelief in his voice.

A set of steely, pale eyes told him that he hadn't succeeded. "I've been asking your father to let me teach you boys for several months now."

Robb wasn't sure that actually answered his question, but he wasn't about to push the issue. For years, Aunt Morcades had just been a name, a vague image in pictures. It wasn't until recently that the kids had even met her. Robb was kind of glad he hadn't known her as a child. She was a bit frightening.

"We're going to start right away. I hope the four of you are in good shape." The sharp look on her face suggested that it wouldn't be good for them if they weren't.

Robb swallowed hard. He had a feeling that Aunt Morcades was going to go well above and beyond what he'd been expecting for self-defense. And he wasn't sure if that was a good thing or not.

It would take four years before he'd find out exactly how far Morcades Durand expected him and his brothers to go, and, by then, he would be grateful for her expertise. What they would face would be like nothing he'd ever imagined possible.

35230094R00126

Made in the USA
Middletown, DE
24 September 2016